After the Burn

Edited by Franklin Ard and Joseph Carro

Published by Rogue Owl Press, 2022.

This is a work of fiction. Similarities to real people, places, or events are entirely coincidental.

AFTER THE BURN

First edition. November 15th, 2022.

ISBN: 979-8-9873401-1-0

BARNING | VERMONT

NORTH

To Goose Mountain

To Geary Mountain

Green River

Provided Courtesy of the Barning News Record

DIRECTORY
1 - Depot
2 - Distillery
3 - Mayor's House
4 - The Wine Library
5 - Barning Graveyard
6 - Church
7 - Apothecary
8 - Barning Orphanage
9 - Town Hall
10 - Barning Bank & Trust
11 - Livery Stables
12 - Court House
13 - Barning News Record
14 - Sheriff's Office & Jail House
15 - Schoolhouse
16 - Lumber Yard
17 - The B.W. General Store
18 - The Silver Blade Saloon
19 - Grist Mill
20 - Doctor's Office
21 - Baseball Field
22 - Bobby's Place
23 - Vacca's Vineyards
24 - Outlying Farms
25 - Ford Ranch

CITY WALL
EDGE OF WOODS
RAILROAD TRACKS
MAJOR STREETS
MINOR STREETS OR FOOT PATHS
x WINE ENTRANCE

WALL GATES

A - WEST GATE ON RAILROAD TRACKS

B - NORTH GATE ON COURT STREET

C - EAST GATE ON DUNBRIDGE STREET

D - EAST GATE ON RAILROAD TRACKS

E - SOUTH GATE ON WARREN STREET

Contents

Introduction

There's something special about Vermont. Growing up in Maine, about a three-hour ride from Vermont at any given time, the state called to me in a way that others didn't. I've spent many years living in or visiting various states in New England, and they all have their draws. I've even spent time living down south in Alabama, and visiting places in Florida, Georgia, Mississippi, and Louisiana. But Vermont is somehow down-to-earth and yet has a mystic quality to it. You could be stuffing your face at a mac and cheese festival, and while you're washing your food down with a craft beer, you look around and realize you're in a mountain valley shrouded with mist. Anything feels possible.

When my good friend, Shane Collins, invited me and our other friend, Franklin Ard, to the aforementioned festival in Vermont back in 2014, I found myself not only surrounded by the hardy mysticism of the Green Mountains, but also in the creative orbit of talented writers who went to grad school with me for creative writing. We were all still closely connected to the Stonecoast MFA program at that point, which is in Maine, and we discussed various stories we had worked on over the previous couple of years. That's when the idea struck me.

Why don't we come up with a shared world setting, which we can use as a sort of creative sandbox that we can all play in with our writing?

I came up with the premise of a sort of "weird west" setting and suggested it be set in post-apocalypse Vermont. We were visiting Montpelier at the time, and I could imagine the town crumbling and the world dying outside of the miraculous bubble within which our fictional city would survive. Then, as Shane drove us to his house in another town in Vermont, I grew more excited at the prospect. The three of us sat in Shane's living room and spitballed various ideas about setting, character, and logistics.

It was decided that Barning would have a core group of established characters that writers involved in the project could reference, but that writers could come up with their own stories using the setting and theme. However, it was envisioned as just a writing exercise at that time. Back in 2014, independent publishing wasn't as professionally accepted or as streamlined, and we didn't imagine the works would be published. A few of us wrote stories, but most forgot about the project because it was just for fun.

But I deeply believed in the potential of Barning, and I kept checking in with people in our group over the years. Then, when Franklin began tinkering with the idea of launching Rogue Owl Press more recently, this project seemed a natural fit for a first publication for the press. He then began the first steps to what you now hold in your hand or e-readers.

Barning is a uniquely weird, tragic, and hopeful place. I hope you have a great time reading about its characters, its history, and its drama. I know we've enjoyed writing all of it.

Joseph Carro

Woodford, Vermont
November 2022

Message from the Barning News Record

The narratives collected herein all take place in or around the town of Barning, Vermont. The words you are about to read paint a picture of how this unique settlement has evolved over a nearly one-hundred-year time span after an apocalyptic event known as *The Burn*, in which tremendous solar flares pummeled the Earth.

Our research here at the *News Record* indicates that the months and years following *The Burn* were (quite literally) a dark period of time known as *The Blackout*, in which the world lost all electrical power—never to be restored. Then there came *The Collapse*, in which society, as it had existed, crumbled due to war, famine, and resource scarcity.

Barning, Vermont, has since become an oasis of sorts, a haven to escape the onslaught from the sun and the dangerous extremes of the outside world. The editors here at the *News Record* hope that, through these narratives, the reader better understands the plight of those who have struggled to survive— and to build a place for themselves and their families to thrive —after the most disastrous events in human history.

Thus, we present to you the frontier town of Barning, Vermont, as seen through the eyes of those who have made their stands here over many decades.

Fortune Favors the Bold

Rebecca McKenna

I don't know when it happened. To say it has always been this way would be a lie. But there was a moment when I realized that the pictures that flashed across my brain were real—or would be real someday.

It wasn't the first time, I'm sure, but early on I had seen a picture in my head of Candy, my cat, sleeping on the floor of the walk-in closet in my parents' bedroom. I had never seen a dead animal before, so I thought it was nice how she lay there, so quiet, letting me pat her. That had been in the vision. When it happened in real life, it wasn't nice.

I had gone into the closet to try on my mom's fancy shoes. I wasn't supposed to, but no one was around. There was Candy, and I bent down to pat her. When she didn't struggle or run away, I tried to pick her up. She was heavy, so much heavier than I imagined she could be. And stiff. And cold. I dropped her and ran to the door of the closet, kicking off the shoes on my way.

I stopped in the door and looked back. Something about that view of the closet brought back the vision. It was déjà vu. It was a memory. It was the future coming to meet the present. It was all of these things, although I didn't have the language to describe it at the time.

The date stamps on the back of pictures of me with Candy stop when I was five, so she must have died around then. At five, I didn't know déjà vu, and I only knew the future as the thing my older cousin Marina talked about. It had something to do with getting married. Later, I would know those things for what they were.

Later, though, the visions clearly became premonitions. And they were right. They were so, so right, and most of the time they weren't happy. And I couldn't stop them. Not to say that they were relentless, but merely that they came far more often than I would have liked, and I couldn't block them out.

Once, during the summer when I was nine, I thought about telling my mom about the pictures. Sometimes they scared me. She thought I had nightmares, and I had never corrected her. I had mulled it over and over in my head for weeks.

We were in Iowa visiting my aunt Cora, and we went to the county fair there. It was so much hotter than I was used to in Vermont. The sky was open, and everything just baked in the sun. I wanted to get into the shade, so I asked if I could go into the fortuneteller's tent. My mom gave me the five dollars, probably just to shut me up. I looked up at the sign advertising Madame Lucia's Magical Emporium and then lifted the curtain flap.

Madame Lucia looked just like I expected her to look. She was an older woman, black hair pulled back and hidden under a scarf. Wide, gold, looped earrings book-ended her fleshy, wrinkled face. Her nose—long, bulbous, and a little crooked—was set squarely between her intense and focused eyes. She wore a floral top and another scarf around her shoulders. As I walked in, she held up a finger of warning to keep me from talking while she gazed into a crystal ball. Beside the ball was a deck of cards.

She looked away from the ball and took up the cards. She asked me to draw one and give it back to her. I did, but I didn't look at it closely. The person on it looked odd. There was some writing on the bottom of the card, but my reading skills weren't great. Besides, I didn't want to take my eyes off of her face.

Madame Lucia finally spoke. She focused all of her attention on me, and her voice was not the creaky, heavily accented voice that I had expected from watching television. It was clear, smooth, and even.

"Don't tell your secret," she said. "Don't tell anyone. Trust no one. Do you understand?"

I nodded but couldn't say anything.

"You don't need to tell me about it," she went on, "because I already know. But I want to tell you to trust yourself. Trust your instinct. Trust your gut. Do you know what that means?"

This seemed a monumental charge, and I didn't understand it. I shook my head.

She reached over and touched my stomach and then my chest. "If something feels right here or here, then trust that feeling, okay?"

That I understood. I nodded.

Madam Lucia leaned back in her chair and looked me over carefully. She sighed. "I could tell you the rest of your fortune, but that would be kind of silly. You will know what's going to happen. At least, you should know the important things. And you'll know what choices are the right ones, okay?"

It was strange, and I felt tingly all over, but I didn't move.

She leaned under her table and pulled out a pack of cigarettes and lit one. My eyes must have betrayed my shock at such reckless behavior because she just laughed. "Your parents probably have told you all about how bad smoking is, huh? And maybe your teachers, too. And they're right. But I'll tell you a little secret. I'm not going to die from lung cancer, and neither are you. Matter of fact, neither of us will ever get any type of cancer. So, if you decide you want to smoke when you grow up, you go right ahead."

Now I was really shocked. Here was an adult telling me to do something bad. But she also made me feel safe. I stayed rooted to the spot even though she had said she wasn't going to tell my fortune.

Madam Lucia continued to exhale in big puffs, filling the room with tobacco smoke. "Maybe you wonder why I told you to keep your secret," she said. "Or maybe you wonder how I know. I can't tell you that. You know. There are some things that you just know. But keeping it secret will keep you safe. Don't be afraid to use what you know, though. That can keep you safe, too." She waved her hand at all of the things cluttered around her tent. There were stuffed snakes, jars of dead spiders, cobwebs, dusty old books, flickering lights, a human skeleton. "None of this is real. I'm telling you though because you are real, and you need to know that you're not alone, okay?"

I nodded one last time.

Madame Lucia held out her hand. "Nice to finally meet you, Rosemary. Have a nice life. Stay out of the sun."

I shook her hand, mumbled thanks, and left. Only as I was approaching my mother did I realize I had never told her my name.

I took the position at the *Barning News Record* when I was just nineteen. Those three college writing classes were enough to qualify me for the job, and I wasn't sure what I wanted to do with my life. I also thought that maybe the visions would be helpful to my career, and I would be the first person on the scene of big stories. But of course, it didn't work that way. I didn't know when things would happen for sure, only that they would. Sometimes I had an idea about what year or season they might happen, but I never had any specific dates. The only time I had a personally beneficial vision, I saw lottery numbers. I played the big three draw games every week for a year. Turns out the numbers were for church bingo. I won $275 dollars.

The *Barning News Record* job wasn't really full-time, so after I'd been there about six months, I opened a fortuneteller's parlor in the building across from the Bowling Blitz and the New New Delhi Restaurant. It helped to pay the bills, and people seemed to like coming in.

I never lied, but I only told half-truths. I told the small stuff. Sometimes I added some drama and gave the messages as veiled warnings. I played to my audience. I did well. And my reputation gave me the courage to ask the *News Record* editor if I could do a horoscope column. He paid me a little more for that, too.

Life was wonderful. I had friends. There was this lively, lovely community. I had my secret, but I had learned to live with it.

Then the big visions began to come. Hellfire and brimstone. Shadows. Bad things. They were crushing. I almost couldn't bear them. I could not publish these in the paper, but I had to write them down to get them out of my head before they made me crazy. I kept them in a green leather journal in my desk drawer. If anyone had ever found them, I would have said they were fanciful, make believe, silly. But I knew the truth.

And I knew I had nowhere to run.

In the parking lot of the Barning Bowling Blitz, he sits on a crumbling Jersey barrier. The Bowling Blitz isn't there anymore, of course. He's not sure when it went away. It might even have been before the Collapse. It might have been after. Either way, now it's just an empty lot. The only reason he knows about it is because of the paper. He's spent years putting together parts and pieces to make a map of before. He has no idea what it was really like. He was still a young boy when the wall was built, when the gates were put up, when the mines were closed. On the map, he places houses in here, a dental office in there based on newspaper records. His map is rough, but it makes him feel better, connected somehow to the people who were here before.

Some nights, he walks by the theatre and admires the lights, the women on the arms of their lovers, the families gathered in the living rooms in front of their televisions. He walks by the New New Delhi and breathes in the curry. At the corner opposite, he almost steps into Madame Rosemerta's Psychic Connection.

He has to imagine all this, though. He was born after The Burn. After The Collapse. After the marquis lights had all busted and after the New New Delhi had gone up in flames. Surely, he must have been born after Madame Rosemerta was long gone.

At least that's what he'd always thought. Madame Rosemerta. He'd seen pictures of her shop sign in the paper archives, and for some reason, he'd always assumed she must have looked like the fortuneteller depicted on the sign. His mother used to tell him bedtime stories about a fortuneteller. In the stories, the fortuneteller was always named Lucia, and she was an old woman with black hair pulled back from her face. She wore heavy gold jewelry and lots of dark clothing. In some of the stories, her eyes were half-hidden by a scarf draped over her head. She gazed into crystal balls and read tarot cards and tea leaves to see into the future. The first time he had seen an old photo of Madame Rosemerta's shop sign, he had assumed that it was where his mother had gotten her description. Stereotypes hadn't gone away with The Collapse—the sign fit his expectation in every way.

Madame Rosemerta's shop had been across the street from the Bowling Blitz. It was empty, and the sign was gone, but part of the house remained. H ecompared what was left t o a p icture f rom the archives. The concrete barrier grew cold as he sat thumbing the edge of the photo. The end of a piece of rebar worried the seam of his pants whenever his weight shifted. In his other hand, he held a second photo. It had fallen from the drawer of a filing cabinet this morning while he was rearranging the *News Record* office.

A young woman, maybe in her late twenties, smiled at the camera. She was what his mother would have called "pretty but plain." Her features were soft, pleasant. He had resisted all day his desire to kiss the picture. The woman held a glass of red wine in one hand and waved to the photographer with the other. He admired the brown hair that curled around her face and marveled that the blue stripes on her shirt complimented the shade of her eyes. It appeared that she was at an informal party. Blurred figures stood in the background.

All day the woman in the photo had held his attention. He'd left the filing cabinet in the middle of the office floor, emptied the drawers in the hopes of finding more pictures. He hadn't cataloged any items today. He hadn't even worked on those wanted posters for the sheriff. Narcissus-like, he'd lost himself in the photo for hours, forgetting even to have lunch. Then he found the green leather journal stuck behind a drawer in an unused desk. He'd read it all.

He looked from the ruins of the building to the picture. He flipped it over, re-reading again the words he'd puzzled over countless times. "Rosemary. 'Madame Rosemerta.' June 2015."

Tucking the photo into the front of the journal, he flipped to the first page and began to read again.

February 22, 2012

I see couples, I think. Two men and two women. Maybe they are cousins or siblings. The men know each other, and the women know each other. I think they are good people, but I don't know any of them. No, wait. That's not right. I know one of the men. At least, I know him as a boy, I believe. He looks so familiar. Like Mr. Ford from the farm, but not quite.

There are two journeys, one short and one longer. And there is bad blood where there should not be. Someone is in danger, but the danger seems to change its target each moment. No one is safe. Trust no one.

March 4, 2012

I can't tell if I am surrounded by love and trust, or by anxiety and jealousy. Maybe all of those are mixed together. But there is definitely adventure. There is a flavor of Tom Sawyer and Huck Finn, but it is modernized. The boys are brothers, I think. And they have a need for speed.

March 29, 2012

There is anger. So much anger. It smells like gunpowder and fire. There is a woman, and she is strong. She is safe. There are men. One of them is already dead, but no one else is to blame for that.

October 13, 2012

I see faces in the dark. They are illuminated by flashes of reflected light as something twirls or spins on occasion, but I don't know what it is. Two men and a woman, and more faces in the dark. Bad faces.

I see Mrs. Vacca, but I do not trust her, which is weird, because she has always been so nice. There are tunnels. Maybe the old mines. I sense choices to be made. Choices about the devil you know versus the devil you don't.

January 14, 2013

Children are survivors. There has been a disaster, and children survive. They gather near the river, and someone takes care of them. "Barning Orphanage" is painted above the door of a large building. It looks like the façade of the women's shelter, but older, more worn. Still, it seems to be the same building. On a knoll, overlooking Green River. Sheltered in some woods. Small orchard off to one side.

The children seem reasonably happy, and yet there is always a feeling of Dickensian moroseness about an orphanage. Never enough food. Never new clothes, always plenty of bullies, always a loss of identity.

June 8, 2013

There is a sickness. It is spreading fast and without regard for who it takes down. There is also a hero. I cannot tell who the hero is, but he seems unlikely. He may be someone who can find his way in the dark. Our unknown hero is missing his father. There are lots of people missing fathers. There is a journey, maybe a journey for more than one person, although they might not be the same journey. There are journeys from darkness into deeper darkness. I believe that at the end of the journeys, there will be answers. There will certainly be light.

June 10, 2013

I recognize the highway coming into Montpelier. It is a long way from Barning, and whoever is on this trip is tired. But there is so much hope. And danger. But overwhelming hope. I have never really liked our capital, but now I feel that I am safe here, and that I could stay forever.

December 20, 2013

How fitting that this is the darkest time of the year. The darkness that I experience isn't a drawing of the veil, nor a clouding of the future, nor a shroud of mystery. It is the darkness of dirt, of cups of dark tea, of graveyards on moonless nights. There are dark men who do dark deeds, and an even darker woman. This is a dream, which is not all a dream. There is a mass of holy things for an unholy usage. Darkness is the universe.

February 3, 2014

The *Barning News Record* office is in my mind. It is empty. Filing cabinets and desks are still scattered around, but there are no people. A cabinet is open. My cabinet. Papers are on the floor in messy piles. Someone has been searching for something. A man comes in the room, and I begin to sweat. This is not a warm glow. It is an honest sweat. My chest and underarms are soaked, and large drops of perspiration are dripping from my forehead down onto my cheeks. I have never seen this man before, but I know him. I know him without question, without doubt. This is my son. And I know that I will love him. And I know that I will lie to him. I will not tell my secret. I will trust no one.

August 1, 2014

I was crossing the tracks, headed for the *News Record*, when Jack Rogers called out my name. The sound of his voice crashed into me, and I almost vomited. Instead, I managed to lift my hand and wave, but when I got over the tracks, I had to sit on a rock to recover. Usually, the visions aren't this clear when they are bad, but they have been more and more so lately. There had been a fireball. There had been lots of them. And then there was television static before flames leapt up everywhere. And I think Jack was hurt. But Jack's pain didn't really matter, because that fire was coming, and it was coming for us all.

Acceptance of Risk

Derek B. Hoffman

Jack woke to the coo of a mourning dove. He hadn't heard one outside his window since Beth passed. He held his eyes closed and sighed. Jack wasn't a sentimental man, but he missed his wife. She died of brain cancer two years before. Every morning without her was torture. This wasn't the retirement he worked so hard for in the Corps.

As he began to roll out of bed, lines of light flashed across the backs of his eyelids. He blinked hard. The trails of white reminded him of shooting stars. He froze, wondering if this was a stroke. He rubbed his eyes. The lines lingered for a moment more before disappearing.

"Not yet, Beth. I have to make sure Will makes it home."

He made his bed before kneeling beside it.

"Please Lord..." It's as far as he got. His mind crowded with memories and her voice. Crystal clear. A breath away. It finished the prayer for him.

Jack smiled and lifted his head. Two photos stood on his nightstand in matching frames. An old picture of Beth. She sat on a rocky ledge, the sea taking a backseat to that beautiful smile. A trip to Maine that had to have been a different life. The other photo was of Will a couple weeks before he shipped off to OCS. His hair was all wild and he had that dimpled grin that caught the eye of too many girls for his own good.

Jack touched the photos before sliding on his running shorts and shoes. He wondered if he was getting soft, old, or just growing up.

Jack took his usual route over trails that snaked through the woods behind his A-frame. Up and down small hills dense with evergreens. The first mile broken only by a property line fence from the 1800s. He could still leap over the stacked stones. He accepted the risk of a fall for that blast of dopamine every morning.

At the end of the second mile, the trail curved next to the two-lane highway that led to the middle of Barning, Vermont. It had been their home since the blizzard that saw them deliver Will on a mattress on the floor by firelight.

As Jack took a left at the town center, he saw his new neighbors getting out of their dinged-up Subaru wagon. Angela was nice enough, but Jack thought her husband was a couple eggs short of a dozen.

Victor had a constant hunch to him. He looked gangly and pudgy at the same time. He dropped a bag of groceries to run to the sidewalk.

"Hey! Hey! Mr. Rogers!"

Dear Lord, please don't let me punch this idiot from New Hampshire.

Victor's face contorted, then turned into a goofy smile. "Mr. Rogers! Will you be my neighbor? Ha! Remember me? It's Vic King. You can call me Victor." He chuckled and held up his hand to give a high five.

Jack stopped in front of him. Looked him in his bloodshot eyes. Jack noticed Angela putting everything back in the dropped grocery bag.

Every one of his sergeant's stripes wanted to shark attack this punk. *Beth, help me breathe. I know I—*

Something smashed through the Subaru's windshield. Angela jumped and dropped the newly packed bag.

Hundreds of starlings fell on the road. It sounded like a cascade of hail. The only thing louder was Victor's screech.

Angela already had her phone out, taking pictures. Jack walked a shaken-up Victor to the passenger seat of their car.

"Can we give you a ride home?" Angela asked.

"No. No," Jack said. Angela's unflinching response to what happened surprised him.

"Can we still count on you for dinner?" Angela asked as she picked up the bird on the console and dropped it outside the car.

Jack found it odd, but he nodded.

Heavy traffic packed I-89 all the way to White River Junction. Jack's thoughts strayed to Will. He would pick him up soon. It would be good to have him home.

Jack parked at a bakery across the road from the VA. He backed his old Hilux into a spot out of habit. He rushed across the street and went into the largest of the many buildings. The way to Dr. Stanley's office had become automatic. Jack just hoped he was available.

He passed the front desk and noticed security in a scuffle with a couple younger vets. He dashed past and took the first staircase to the fourth floor. Two steps at a time, he didn't breathe hard.

The sterile corridor of offices zigged and zagged. He finally reached 1428A. He knocked twice.

"Come in."

"Dr. Stanley," Jack said as he extended his hand.

"Jack! So good to see you!" Dr. Stanley stood, pulled his sweater neat, and shook the offered hand. "How are you? Especially with all that's going on."

"You heard about the birds in Barning?"

Dr. Stanley shook his head while he took a sip of coffee. "Oh, there have been events all over New England. Probably beyond. Cell networks. GPS. We've had trouble with some of our machines. Hell, Dartmouth had some crazies trying to steal the magnet out of one of their MRIs!"

"What?!" Jack couldn't believe any of it.

"I know. Those magnets are about fifteen to twenty tons!" Dr. Stanley chuckled. "They were going to put it in their little pickup."

"I—"

"I'm sorry, Jack. I went off. What's got you coming in today? I've got about ten minutes before my next appointment, but they are all yours."

"Thank you, Dr. Stanley. I appreciate that. I appreciate all you've done for me, for Beth, for Will." Jack paused with a deep breath. "I'm seeing lights when I close my eyes. It just started this morning. Bright lines. They went away, at first. Now they won't."

Dr. Stanley nodded. "Good news and bad news for you. The good news is that you aren't alone. Many people are seeing what you described. Just about everyone I've talked to, as a matter of fact. Bad news is that it's cosmic rays."

Jack sighed and rubbed his head with the palm of his hands. "This doesn't make sense. Really—cosmic rays?"

Dr. Stanley shifted in his seat and shuffled a stack of folders into another pile. "I don't know either. I have some suspicions. People above my pay grade have been talking to people in D.C. and elsewhere. We have a former astronaut as a patient. His doc told me that the last time he saw these lights was when he was outside the ISS."

"Are you kidding, Dean?" Jack asked.

"I wish I was. I have to get going soon, Jack. What was the other thing?"

"Will?"

Dr. Stanley tightened his face. "He's ready. If you go to Building Two. I'll make a quick call and they can have someone walk him out to you."

"That would be great. Thank you, Dean. God bless you and the work you do here."

"Thanks, Jack. Good luck. It was good seeing you again. Stay safe out there."

Jack knew he wouldn't see Dr. Stanley again. But Will was almost home.

He retrieved the Hilux and pulled in front of Building Two. A Lieutenant escorted Will. Jack signed some paperwork, helped strap Will into his seat, and hit I-89 north.

Neither of them spoke. Jack wanted to say something, but the words weren't right yet.

Beth wore a pink top and blue jeans. Her bare feet held her to the rock. She smiled as the sun hit her. The sea breeze made it cold that day. Two islands framed a sailboat in the distance. The waves crashed, covering all other sounds. She was positively giddy.

Jack saw her highs and lows in the years that followed. He saw her golden hair turn from blonde to brown to gray to when it fell out from the chemo and radiation. No matter what she wore or how she felt, he always saw the echo of that day around her.

The hiss of steam from the iron snapped Jack from his reverie.

"Shit!" He pulled the iron up from his burning, brown-stained white shirt.

He decided on a blue Polo shirt to go with his light gray slacks. He slipped on black loafers and his old Timex. Jack looked at the drawer that held his ankle holster and .38. Strange days were upon all of them, but he could hear Beth telling him to be calm.

The bottle of wine, shortbread, strawberries, and whipped cream sat bundled in the refrigerator. He tried to tie a ribbon around them all like Beth did, but he gave up and put it all in one of the many nice gift bags from Beth's side of the closet. He carefully folded wrapping paper on top.

"Will, I'll only be gone for a bit." Jack paused, wanting to say more. He left in silence.

As he walked up his neighbors' drive, Jack noticed someone had meticulously completed the landscaping. It looked like the "after" videos of the home show he'd watch on Sunday evenings with Beth. But as he took a closer look, he noticed garden gnomes in oddly strategic positions in the bushes and trees. If he looked just right, he saw the glint of light off five security cameras hidden amongst the gnomes.

Jack shook his head, took a deep breath and smelled juniper. Another reminder of who he had lost. *Too many today*, he thought. He steadied himself on the porch and pushed the emotions aside. Before he could knock on the door, Angela opened it broadly and smiled at him. Though she wore the right look, something in her eyes gave Jack pause.

He handed her the gift bag with wine and the makings for strawberry shortcake. She led him to their living room with a TV as big as the wall on one side and a plush leather sectional on the other. As news reports from around the world flashed across the large screen, upbeat Latin music played too loudly from the kitchen.

"Can I help?" Jack asked.

"Oh no, I've got this. There's some Cabot and crackers on the coffee table. And Vic opened a nice Cab from Vacca's. Sit back, enjoy the news."

Jack noticed her navy dress with little dots and a matching cardigan. Beth would have adored her outfit. But her words hung in his mind, and he sat uneasily on the ottoman while having some appetizers.

Tensions around the globe mount as information leaks from NASA, ESA, and JSA about the magnetosphere all but disappearing during one of the worst solar storms ever recorded.

Jack felt dizzy as the sounds grew together—the clashing of pans, the syncopated beats and bells from the music, and the newscasts and ads. He wasn't sure if it was his service or age that caused the confusion, but he felt like he needed some air.

Victor rapped him on the shoulder. "Hey, thank you for being my neighbor! And thanks for coming!"

Jack sighed and put on a smile as he turned to face his host. "Hello! Quite the place you have here. I like all the gadgets."

"Oh, I've got some other stuff you're going to love. C'mon. Follow me." Victor wore a too-tight cardigan and chinos. A slightly stained T-shirt bulged out. Something changed about his neighbor's demeanor. He carried himself differently.

Jack followed the large strides of his host to a slightly lower level. Victor swung open French doors to a room that was lit by multi-colored tiles, light strips, and Jack wasn't even sure about the rest. It all centered around three screens of a computer and another larger screen above. He could see perimeter camera feeds, lines of black and white scrolling upward, different news stations showing large blasts in the middle of the French and Costa Rican countrysides. Fields in China burned.

Victor whistled. "Hey! Over here, man!"

Jack pulled himself away. "What happened?"

"You haven't seen? Jesus, she was right, you really are in your own little world. It's the end times. We're just seeing how bad it's going to get. Or maybe not. Ha!"

Jack suddenly wished he had brought his gun.

"Alright, so this is some cool shit," Victor said as he opened a drawer and pulled out a leather folder. "Check out these coins. Could be the currency of the new world order, bro."

Victor laid out a collection of mint condition Chuck E. Cheese tokens. Before Jack could respond, Victor was already opening the next drawer. "Or, or, or, check this!"

In a glass display case were a series of smoothed rocks like the ones Beth liked to pick from beaches they visited, but they all had little knit hats on them.

"Beauties, aren't they? Ange thinks I'm crazy, but I know one day we'll have a little girl who will treasure these." Victor cleared his throat and spit in a trash can he pulled from under the desk with all the screens. "But what I really wanted to show you in particular were these."

He unlocked and opened a cabinet. Inside were the worst made guns in the world.

"Like my AR? It's an American Tactical 9mm. I also have it in 5.56. These are my handgun babies. Another ATI .45 Auto. My Taurus G3. All top shelf, am I right?" Victor smiled and sat smugly in his computer chair.

"What is this? All of it is shit. The coins are worthless. I'm not even talking about the rocks, and these guns are all shoddy. They either break down after a thousand rounds or rust out. What are you playing—"

A blaring tone cut across all of the speakers in the house. It was an Emergency Broadcast message stating that flares were imminent.

"Oh Jesus!" Angela yelled as she looked at her phone then out the window over the kitchen sink. "Oh no. No!"

The power went out.

"Ange? What's going on, Ange? C'mon. Come here. Come here!"

Jack pulled out the mini flashlight on his keychain. He glimpsed a pudgy tear-soaked face turning red in anger.

"ANGE! Get over here! I need you now!"

Angela lit a candle and brought it over to the end table by Victor's shaking form. "Just a moment, dear. We have a guest."

As she moved away, Victor's hand snaked around her wrist and yanked her backwards. "You will stay right here."

Victor's voice reminded Jack of the Major General's that got him busted down. He was an asshole too. Jack was about to do something that would get him in trouble again, but then he remembered—

"Will!"

Jack turned and ran out the door. He hoped he wasn't too late. As he neared the property line, he felt a sharp pain in the back of his head. He saw the world tunnel to black as he fell.

Jack?

Jack. Wake up.

"Beth?"

I need you.

"I'm sorry, honey. I can't see or move."

I need you, Jack. Please, wake up!

"I...I can't. Beth, I'm sorry."

She needs you, Jack. Get up. You're not finished, Marine.

"Beth—"

"My name's Angela. Remember? Your neighbor?"

Lines of light poured across his eyelids. They fluttered open. Jack saw shapes then colors. It was horribly bright. Her face came into focus. Scrapes and a black eye.

She helped him sit up. He coughed up something bloody. Angela held a cloth to the back of his head. Her other hand covered his heart. A ring of bruises and cuts circled her wrist. Jack looked up at her face.

She sighed. "He went crazy. He ran after you, grabbed a hammer from a shelf, and—"

"It's okay," Jack said. "If things are as bad as it seems, everyone's going to act a bit out of sorts."

"No. He's fucking evil. That big shit hit me before. He has controlled me since California and he—now he needs to die," Angela said as she helped Jack stand.

"Where is he now?"

"I don't know. He took your truck. I'm guessing he took whatever else was useful that you had."

"How long ago did he leave?" Jack asked.

"Not long. He...he took Will."

A throbbing behind Jack's eyes. The white lines bright and pulsing. "Did the flare hit?"

She shook her head.

"Okay. Pack some rugged clothes, whatever supplies you can find. I'm going to change and grab a few things and meet you back here."

She nodded. "My family is out camping. I don't know if they know what's going on. They are supposed to be on Goose Mountain, just north of town."

"Understood." Jack hobbled back to his house.

He kicked on the generator and pump to take a quick shower. While he put on his old hunting gear, Jack turned on the radio for local information. He found his .38 and Will's old Remington 1187 in his closet as he learned about the Vancouver fireball and thousands of failing satellites.

Jack took the photos of Beth and Will out of their frames and put them in his left breast pocket. He collected his go-bag and a couple waters. He paused in the doorway.

"God please bless whoever steps foot in this house next. Thank you for all you gave me here." A final sigh before he met Angela next door.

She had the Subaru running and stocked with supplies. She leaned against the door wearing a black sweater and jeans. "I was about to come check on you."

Jack nodded. "Just saying—"

The shockwave knocked them both to the ground.

Something set the sky ablaze. To the north, a growing plume of dust and ash glowed red and black.

"Get in the car!" Jack yelled.

Angela had it in gear and they tore onto the road. "Where am I going?"

"Get to that parking garage by Bailey's Pub and that art supply place."

"Got it." Angela floored the Subie. She took corners like a natural born racer, finding the best line every time. "Let me know if it's too fast."

"No. Fast is good," Jack said as he clutched the door.

"Did you see where it hit?" Angela asked.

"Yes. It hit Goose," Jack couldn't lie.

They swerved around a crashed car. She drifted the wagon on the outside curve, almost hitting a dazed cyclist.

"Do you need to stop?" Jack asked.

"No." She gritted her teeth and sped up. "We don't know anything. And we have to stay alive to get that bastard."

The ashy dirt began falling on Barning. "It's making the road greasy. Does that garage have speed bumps?"

"I don't remember," Jack said.

"Alright. This might be a rough stop." Angela slid off of Main and onto Temple Street. The opening for the garage stood before them.

"Veer right to go down. I'm worried about the heat."

The Subaru tore off the security arm. Angela spun the wheel to the right. The car lost its driver-side mirror to the interior wall. "Two levels?"

"Should do."

They parked. Angela pried her hands from the steering wheel.

"You did great," Jack said.

She looked at him, on the verge of crying, "Thank you."

Jack touched her shoulder and looked in her eyes. "Now it's my turn. I'm taking my pack up a level to check for a LoJack signal from my Hilux. I'll also scan for emergency radio. I will listen for safe spots and survivors."

Jack pulled the .38 from his ankle holster and made sure the cylinder was full. Angela took it and sighted it.

"You've shot before." It wasn't a question.

"My dad. He took me to a friend's house. We shot at old steel rims he hung at 3, 7, and 15 yards," Angela said.

"I'll try to be back in ten to fifteen minutes. Keep the car running."

"Roger that," she said.

Jack found the Hilux right away. Victor parked or abandoned it at a state forest south of town, heading toward New Hampshire. Jack hadn't been there since before Will left for OCS. They'd gone fishing at the lake, but only found sunfish and mosquitoes.

The CB and portable HAM radios had nothing but static. Jack tuned to CB Channel 9 to transmit.

"Mayday. Mayday. Mayday. This is Barning, Vermont. Unidentified object hit Goose Mountain. It's on fire and TARFU. Is anybody listening? Over."

Jack repeated the message on VHF Channel 16 in case anyone was listening on the lakes or rivers. It was illegal to do from land, but he figured that didn't matter much anymore.

He gave up after ten minutes and turned off the radios to conserve battery.

Angela was out of the car, using it as cover, when Jack walked down the ramp. He held his hands up.

"Anything?" she asked.

"I found the truck, but nothing on the radio. It's probably the debris and whatever is going on up there." He waved his hand toward the sky.

"What do you think we should do?" She offered the gun back to him, but he shook her off.

"Keep it. I want to get to the truck. I hope Will is—"

"Get in. Let's finish this."

Jack thought about arguing to keep her safe, but he knew she was probably more capable than he was at his age. "You know it might go bad, right?"

She looked around and held her hands out. "I think it's pretty fuckin' bad right now."

"Good point."

As they sped out of town, they saw brown ash everywhere. Goose Mountain smoldered a dull red in the rearview mirror.

"Tell me about Will," Angela said.

"Ever since he was little, he's been fascinated with how things work. Kids ask questions, but he asked all of them, and he remembered all the answers." Jack looked out his window. Blankets of ash formed near the tops of the evergreens. It looked like the salted, dirty snow that would collect on the sides of the roads in March. "As he grew up, the questions about how things worked turned to how people worked. He loved everyone he met. Genuinely. He smiled and had this way about him. Especially with girls, but really, it's everyone. That love for people turned into a love for country and the freedoms we have."

"What...what happened?"

"I actually tried talking him out of joining. I know what that life can do to a person. War is one thing, but there are so many other dynamics that people don't understand unless you are in it. I didn't want him to blindly follow his heart to something that could break it so completely." Jack made fists with his hands and stretched them out. His chest felt tight. "I got busted down from an E-7, which is a Gunnery Sergeant, to just a Sergeant because I spoke up to the officer that got a lot of good men killed."

Angela dodged some debris on the road, the tires skidding in the greasy ash.

"Will...he did more than that. He was at an outpost. It came under attack. No reinforcements because it was in the worst position. He saw his best friend get shot in the head by a sniper. Most people, and I thought he might be one of them, would rightly freeze, be scarred, and live in that moment. But whatever happened tore something loose. He grabbed his friend's gun and ammo and became what most warriors only dream to be when forced to fight. He had twenty-five kills and rallied the rest of the troops to action."

"Jack, you don't—"

"Even though they turned the tide, the sniper was still out there. Will got shot dead center, right through his heart." He put the heels of his palms to his eyes. "I'm happy for the survivors, the ones...he is a hero to their families...but I'd rather have him home. I'd rather be able to see the rest of his life." Jack held back the tears like he had for the past month. Pushed them deep into his gut. Pushing them into a ball, dark and lethal.

"I'm so sorry. I thought—"

"Let's just find that son of a bitch."

"Take the second left. There used to be a maintenance shed we can park the car behind. It will be in a blind from the road and the trailhead," Jack said.

Angela backed in the Subaru. Before getting out, she handed a key to Jack. "It's the spare, in case I don't make it back."

"I'll give it back in a few hours." Jack loaded the shotgun with saboted slugs and grabbed his bag.

"We're not good on range," Angela said. "We're going to have to be quiet."

Jack nodded. "The truck is parked at the end of the second parking lot. We proceed carefully, stay near the tree line. The ash is a little less here, and I'm hoping we can catch a track or two. Is he outdoorsy at all?"

Angela laughed. "No. He's allergic to the sun."

"Good. Let's get moving. If my watch is still correct, it is mid-afternoon."

They walked quickly from their blind to the opposite tree line. The first parking lot had a Honda Civic with its side smashed in and the blinker flashing. Jack noticed the ash falling harder.

As they approached the next parking lot, they saw the Hilux at the trailhead. Smoke rose from the engine. Victor must have run it into one of the wooden posts.

Jack signaled to Angela that he would move ahead toward the pickup. She nodded.

He could see the outline of a tilted head. He hunched low and skirted the bed on the passenger side, staying clear of the side mirror's view.

Jack looked back at Angela, barely visible against the darkened trees. She had the .38 drawn and pointed at the truck. He took a breath and counted down on his fingers—three, two, one—

He popped up as he opened the door.

"Boo!" Victor yelled, smiling at him.

Jack felt the bullet before he heard it. The force spun him around and down. His left shoulder became useless.

He heard Victor laughing. "Nice shot, honey! Do you want me to finish him or just take his stuff? His house is going to be so sweet!"

Jack had fallen to the ground but was able to reach the shotgun he had dropped. He held it tightly in his right hand, his finger on the trigger, waiting, steadying his breath.

Victor stepped out of the truck. A shotgun blast obliterated his right foot. He screamed and crumpled to the ground. Jack fired again into the young man's hip. The accompanying screech was both horrible and satisfying.

Another bullet hit Jack in his left arm. Angela ran toward the truck. Jack aimed low and fired at her legs.

"Missed. One left. Better make it count, old man," she said from behind the rear driver's side wheel.

Jack was losing too much blood.

I'm here, Jack. It's not time yet. Pull it together. Get Will where he needs to go.

He shot to the right of the tire.

"Oops. All out, Jack." Angela walked around the tailgate. She aimed Jack's own revolver at his head. "Goodbye. You were sweet. And gullible. And dumb as—"

The slug hit her in the gut. She stumbled back then doubled over.

"I had one in the chamber," he said. Jack took off his belt and made a tourniquet. He pulled himself up with his other hand. The box with Will's ashes sat on the backseat. He moved it to the front seat, retrieved his gun from Angela's twitching hand, and started the truck. He backed over Angela's body with two big thumps.

Jack drove to the cemetery by the First Baptist Church of Barning. A thick, surreal blanket covered the sanctuary. He staggered out of the truck, almost falling into a foot of ash. Wading through the brown-grey mess took all his strength.

Four rows back, five markers to the left. He cleared off her headstone with his jacket sleeve.

He curled up, holding the box that contained the last of his family. He reached out and touched her name on the marker.

"I got him, Beth. I got him home."

Relics

Chloe Viner

Those first childhood memories,
old film on a spool
no color, splotchy sound...
a merry go round of what used to be
where you taught me to play croquet
with the old wooden set
before I knew that wood rots
and people die

This boat is a relic of days past
when things were made to last
your love the yellow lines
on the highway directing everyone
visible even in starless nights
my love this canoe
oars parting the waves
sunlight on the back of my neck
hull still leakproof
after all these years

The Finders

Shane R. Collins

Jules Stetson and Chuck Ford sat in rocking chairs on the porch of Bobby's Place, sipping beer from Mason jars and watching the blue sky over Goose Mountain turn orange and red. Chuck rested his feet on an empty stool. Jules rocked slowly, the old wooden chair creaking in protest. The beer was black and sour. Not one of Bobby's best, but better than the swill they served at Lucy's Tavern on Main Street. It wasn't known as Lucy's Tavern. The sign out front said *Silver Blade Saloon,* but Jules never called it that because when he tried, he felt like a reluctant participant in a game of Dungeons and Dragons. It didn't matter because he rarely went to Lucy's anyway. Too much riffraff. Drunks and gamblers, families passing through, and scrawny men looking to trade work for a meal. Lucy's was for visitors, while Bobby's was for the locals.

Chuck took a noisy sip and cringed.

"Least it's cooling down outside," Jules said and touched the sweating Mason jar to his forehead. It was mid-August and the thermometer had hovered above 100 degrees over the past five days. The afternoons were scorching, the nights steamy and smothering, but Jules and Chuck had seen worse. Rain was a distant memory, and Jules felt like he hadn't slept in days. He finished his drink and looked at Bobby across the porch. Bobby had lost an eye in a knife fight a few years back. As a favor, Jules had searched everywhere for a glass eye. In the end, he found a marble containing an entombed butterfly that was a perfect fit.

34

It was unsettling to see a monarch butterfly where Bobby's iris should have been, but Jules got used to it over time.

Bobby disappeared inside the house and returned a minute later with a pitcher of ice-cold beer, which he kept in an old fridge powered by a scavenged solar panel.

"Add it to the tab," Jules said, and Bobby smiled politely at the tired joke. A few years back, Jules and Chuck had ransacked an abandoned brewery and hauled back a couple of wooden barrels and a thirty-gallon brew kettle for Bobby. It had taken three days to drag the stainless-steel contraption onto an old trailer and wheel it back with the aid of a team of oxen. Bobby hadn't had anything for payment except to promise "free beer for life." Chuck and Jules had taken him up on that.

Locating and hauling random junk back to Barning was how Jules and Chuck made a living. Chuck had inherited Ford Ranch, a small dairy farm that also had chickens and grew corn and wheat, and in the hills above their farmhouse stood the remnants of the old orchard. Jules helped Chuck with odd jobs around the ranch. He helped plow the fields in the spring and carried buckets of grain in the fall. The rest of the time, the two men got the things the people of Barning needed. Not the average things like food and lumber and clothes. The general store in town handled those. Jules and Chuck got the more exotic merchandise.

Bolts of dyed cotton cloth and breeding livestock from traders who carried goods up the Connecticut River on wooden rafts. Spare parts for tillers and horse-drawn carts. Bicycle pumps and black powder rifles. Stephen King novels and sets of Monopoly and checkers for Christmas. Fireworks in the summer. When famine had wiped out a whole harvest of corn and carrots, Jules and Chuck disappeared for a week and returned with a wagonload of flour and a hundred jars of pickles. During the plague five years back, they'd ridden north to Burlington, to an honest-to-God hospital, and returned with a sack of antibiotics.

They'd found a decade's worth of *Popular Mechanics* for the library and were always on the hunt for copies of *Playboy* for the General Store. They'd gotten stethoscopes and glass vials for the doctor and some stainless-steel throwing knives for Lucy. A couple years back, they spent a whole month tracking down a couple of potted cactuses for Tamila's apothecary. Had they known the cactuses were for making peyote, they would have charged double.

Jules and Chuck got the items that no one thought existed anymore. Rifle cartridges and Army boots for Sheriff Bethany and her deputies. Boxes of condoms. A generator that ran on wood gas. Once, when scouring a long-abandoned Costco, they spent half a day clearing away moldy drywall and cracked ceiling tiles from a section where the ceiling had collapsed. Underneath, they found a few hundred rolls of toilet paper. When they returned to Barning, the town had gathered along Dunbridge Street, hailing them as victorious heroes.

They also obtained things that required discretion. Prostitutes for Mayor Amos' house parties. Two ounces of heroin for the town priest. OxyContin and dynamite for Montgomery Fulbright, the town idiot. They didn't ask Monty what the drugs and explosives were for, and, in turn, Monty didn't ask where they had found them. People rarely wanted to know where their purchases came from, as long as they got what they wanted. So far, nothing in town had exploded.

"I hear Chuck's horse barn is nearly ready," Bobby said. "You finally going to put down some roots soon?"

"You don't want me moving in next door," Jules said. "I'll throw parties that'll keep you up all night."

Bobby laughed. "Can't be no worse than Amos."

Last winter, an oil lantern had caught fire in Chuck's horse barn across the road from Bobby's Place. Jules and Chuck had sprinted barefoot half a mile across the pasture to save the horses and put out the fire. The structure survived intact, but the interior needed to be gutted. Rather than restoring it in the spring, Chuck had instead decided to expand another barn to hold the horses. He decided the second barn was too much and had begun fixing it up into a house to sell, though it was clear from the start he had one buyer in mind. Chuck had been trying to sell it to Jules all summer. The gold wasn't a problem. Eighteen ounces was a lot, but he had almost thirty ounces saved in an old ammo canister buried in the graveyard. Business in Barning was good. Jules had so far resisted, but he was beginning to forget why.

"Course, if you ain't interested, I might be," Bobby said. Since Chuck began renovating the barn, Bobby had been sniffing after it like a bat going after a cow with a nick on its ear. "Might be I could turn that old barn into a proper flop house."

"Bet you could, Bobby."

Jules noticed someone walking up the road toward Bobby's Place. It was a woman, though he couldn't tell at first. She wore rags - pieces of clothing torn apart and resown—and in some cases tied—together. She must have been around fifty. Her face was brown with grime and dust. Her dark, oily hair was tied back into a thin ponytail. When she stepped up to the porch, Jules saw that her eyes were bloodshot.

"I'm looking for The Finders," she whispered. Her voice was hoarse, as if she were unaccustomed to using it.

Chuck stood up first. He took off his faded cowboy hat and wiped at the sweat spilling down his forehead. Jules had always wanted to make fun of Chuck's hat but could never bring himself to. Chuck had made it himself, literally skinning the bull and tanning the hide. It was hard to call someone corny when they went through that much trouble.

Jules stood too and took off his green and white baseball cap that was covered in appalling stains. Embroidered on the front was a green serpent, the mascot for the Vermont Lake Monsters.

Chuck held out his hand. "Name's Chuck, Ma'am."

The woman seemed frightened by the gesture but surprised Jules by shaking.

"Jules," he said and nodded. He didn't make her shake his hand too.

The woman cleared her throat. "My name's Sarah." Her voice had a girlish undertone. Jules was beginning to think he'd misjudged her age. She might have actually been a decade and a half younger than he and Chuck—maybe thirty or so. Sarah may have been beautiful, if only she could wash up, sleep in a bed, and eat a few hot meals.

Jules turned toward Bobby. "What's Dot got in the kitchen?"

"Barley soup."

"We'll take three bowls."

Chuck gestured to the stool on which he'd been resting his boots, and Sarah sat down.

"I need your help." She motioned in the direction of the town. "Folks say you two can find anything."

"Folks do say that." Chuck put his cowboy hat back on and sat down.

"What can we find for you?" Jules asked.

"My sister," Sarah said.

Jules and Chuck exchanged looks. They were experts at tracking down things, not people.

"That's..." Chuck said and paused, the 's' lingering like cigarette smoke. "...really not what we do."

"Please, you have to help me."

"Have you asked Sheriff Bethany?" Jules asked.

"She said she can't help because I'm not a resident. She was the one who told me to come see you two."

Jules sighed with annoyance. Bethany could forget about those shotguns she'd asked him to track down. The porch creaked as Bobby approached, carrying a tray with three bowls of steaming soup. He set them on a small end table next to them. Sarah picked up a spoon on the tray and, tentatively at first, sipped the soup. After a couple bites, she gained momentum, slurping it down faster.

"Why don't you tell us what happened?"

Sarah licked her lips and a clean spot appeared on her chin where the broth had washed away some of the filth.

"We were traveling along the interstate to our parents' house. They had a place in Manchester, and we were hoping to get there before the first frost. One night, we were camping on the side of the road and when I woke the next morning, she was gone. Disappeared. Her sleeping bag was still there." Sarah's voice strained, and she began talking faster, as if trying to get it out before she fell apart. "Someone must have taken her. Marauders or outlaws. I don't know. But you have to save her. I can only imagine what—" Sarah stopped there and let out a single, violent sob.

Chuck kept a small notebook and pencil in his pocket and took it out. Whenever he and Jules took a job, he jotted down the details. Jules gave him a scornful look, but Chuck shrugged sheepishly and started writing. The journal and pencil were luxury items. Chuck had a whole stash of writing supplies back at the farmhouse. He could have sold a couple of pencils and bought a week's worth of food, but he didn't because he had aspirations of being a writer. Back when they'd been sophomores at UVM, Chuck had been an English major. Chuck was stubborn, the kind of guy who wouldn't let something like the end of the world ruin his dreams.

When she calmed down a minute later, Chuck asked Sarah about her sister. Her name was Clare. She was twenty, thin, had brown hair and blue eyes. A crescent-shaped scar on her forehead curved from her left eyebrow to the temple. No tattoos. Clare's favorite meal was green beans and potatoes fried in bacon fat. Their mother gave Clare a necklace of a laminated peacock feather that she always wore. She was allergic to pollen and green peppers—not red or orange or yellow peppers, just the green ones. Some years back, a boy who liked Clare had chased her with a stick. She'd thrown a brick at him and had fortunately missed. That was the kind of girl she was. At some point, Chuck stopped taking notes. Jules began to steer the conversation to their finder's fee, which the woman clearly wouldn't be able to pay, but Chuck interrupted him, asking Sarah whether she enjoyed her food. Jules cut him a look, but Chuck made a slight gesture at Sarah and nodded.

There was a hotel in Barning, but Jules wasn't sure Sarah would be able to make it back. Her eye lids drooped. The skin was taut around her cheeks and collarbone. Bobby had a couple of spare rooms. She accepted the invitation to stay, thanked them, and they said goodnight to her.

As they walked along the rutted dirt path to the ranch, Chuck said, "We're doing this one for free, aren't we?"

"We shouldn't be taking this one at all," Jules said. "We don't find people. There's never any money in it, and it never turns out well. I promise you, that girl is dead. We'll be lucky if we come back in one piece ourselves"

Chuck shook his head. "It is the right thing to do."

"Bullshit. I know why you want to do it."

Chuck smirked and looked away. "There's no women like her in Barning."

Jules took a deep breath and lit a cigarette. "This is stupid. We're going to get killed because you want a girlfriend. And don't tell me this is the *right thing to do* like you're suddenly some moral paragon."

Neither one of them spoke as they walked back home. When their house was in sight, Jules flicked his cigarette at a tree stump. "If we do this, I'm calling the shots."

Chuck grinned and gave him a mock salute.

That night, Jules had a familiar dream. He stood in a field. Stalks of golden grain swayed in a breeze he couldn't feel, rustling like a saltshaker. Was it wheat or barley? The sun was warm on the back of his head and shoulders. He brushed his palms over the tops of the grain. He smelled cow manure and the electric scent of a coming storm.

The next morning, Chuck and Jules saddled up a pair of horses and rode out of town. An hour after dawn, the sun was already scorching, heat radiating from the pavement. Jules wiped sweat from his forehead as he bobbed on the trotting horse. He had never quite gotten used to horseback riding. He preferred his bicycle. The bicycle didn't need hay or water. He never worried about the bicycle breaking its leg. His bicycle didn't have teeth. It was lightweight, easy to stash if they needed to hide, and faster on the rutted highways that spanned Vermont. But they had no idea where Clare might be, and the horses were better for rugged backcountry.

A month ago, a buckle on Jules' saddlebag had broken. Since they might be gone for a few days, he stopped by Barning's general store, the BW. There were a half-dozen saddlebags to choose from, and he picked the largest. He gave Ben Warren, the proprietor, a pair of silver coins. Ben accepted the coins and asked, "You finally leaving us?"

It was an old joke. Jules planned to go back home to Iowa, but since it hadn't happened yet, the townsfolk thought he never would. "Not today," Jules said.

Outside, he secured the saddlebags to his chestnut mare, Molly. Sitting atop his own horse, Chuck handed Jules a backpack of supplies. A few apples, a loaf of bread, beef jerky, some water bottles, bullets and black powder, and a wool blanket.

"Ready partner?" Chuck asked. Chuck held a shotgun in one hand, the barrel resting on his shoulder. They both wore leather pistol belts, black powder revolvers holstered in them.

"Don't do that," Jules said and hoisted himself into Molly's saddle.

Chuck adjusted his cowboy hat and shouted, "Yeehaw!" Chuck spurred his horse, and Molly went galloping after him.

Around midday, after stopping to rest the horses only once, Jules and Chuck came to the area where Sarah said Clare had vanished. A sleeping bag still marked the spot. Hadn't Sarah thought to take it? Jules supposed she was barely strong enough to carry her own pack.

Chuck crouched near the spot. He adjusted his hat to block out the harsh sunlight. Jules stayed on the horse, keeping watch. Whoever had taken Clare might still be around. They might think two half-assed cowboys would be an easy target. Chuck brushed his fingers over the matted vegetation Wild mint and goldenrod, mostly. Jules rolled his eyes. If Chuck had any talent for tracking, he'd hidden it all these years.

Finally, Chuck stood up and said, "I don't see anything."

Jules shifted on his saddle, oiled leather creaking under him. "Quabbin's just three miles ahead."

Chuck grimaced. "Even if they know something, they ain't telling us shit."

"Worth a try, just the same."

Chuck got back on his horse, and the two men started down the road.

As they neared Quabbin, pine and spruce trees gave way to maple and birch. The road sloped downhill as they approached the intersection. After The Collapse, a group of tourists, businessmen, and college students—all out-of-towners—took over what was once a campground called Quabbin State Park. They built log cabins on tent sites. They fished the lake, hunted the woods, and cleared fields for crops. It was a quiet, peaceful community whose inhabitants were perennially mistrusted and labeled as outsiders by folks in Barning.

A watchtower marked the entrance to Quabbin. The structure's thick pine timbers made Jules wonder if its engineer had learned architecture from Lincoln Logs.

"You should stay back," Jules said.

Chuck nodded his consent.

Jules, an out-of-towner himself, had the best chance of dealing with those in Quabbin.

Molly's hooves *clop-clop-clop*ped on the uneven pavement as Jules neared the settlement. The gate—a scrap metal quilt of street signs, garbage can lids, and rusted tin roofs bolted and lashed together—swung open. The leader of the community, a man named Chase, approached Jules. Jules had done jobs for Chase on a couple of occasions. What had Jules gotten for him? Some hacksaws and axes? It had been a while.

Jules held up his hand to assure Chase that he was unarmed. Chase, wearing a cloth poncho with a rope belt, waved back.

When he was only a few yards away, Jules jumped down from his horse. Best not to be looking down on Chase. Chase had a reputation for being sensitive that way.

"What brings you here?" Chase asked.

"Looking for a girl," Jules said, taking a few steps closer to Chase. He saw movement on the watchtower. A man held a scoped rifle, not aimed at Jules, but close. "Name's Clare. About twenty. Blue eyes, brown hair."

Chase nodded and chewed on a wad of tobacco. Jules couldn't tell whether the nod meant that Chase knew something. Jules kept talking. "Went missing a couple nights back. Sister wants us to track her."

"You know what I've been thinking lately?" Chase asked but didn't wait for a response. "Football. Four quarters. First and ten. Touchdown and the point after. I'd split a twelve pack with my brother-in-law every Sunday. You used to watch football? I bet there must have been some Iowan college team you liked." Jules recalled that Chase used to be an investment banker or something. He couldn't even remember what that meant. Now, he looked more like an oarsman two years deep into the Lewis and Clark expedition. Cold gray eyes, callused hands, a beard that hadn't felt a razor in months.

"I was more of a baseball guy," Jules said and pointed to his Lake Monsters cap.

Chase laughed. "Never had the patience for baseball."

Jules nodded. Better to let Chase take his time.

"During the offseason, I'd count the days to the preseason. Shit, I even watched the draft. I remember that I did it, that I loved it, even remember how the game worked. But hard as I try, I can't recall a single pass, run, or touchdown. Weird, right? Twenty years is a long time."

Jules nodded and waited for him to say something relevant.

Chased chewed his tobacco for a few seconds and spit at a pile of leaves. "A missing girl, huh? We had a couple kids go missing last year. Asked Sheriff Bethany to help us out. You know what she said?"

"That you weren't residents so she wouldn't help."

"That whole town is chickenshit," Chase said. "Why the hell should I help you when you wouldn't lift a finger?"

"Should've come to Chuck and me. We'd have helped you."

"Bullshit."

"We're cut from the same cloth," Jules said. "I'm an outsider, same as you."

"Still planning on going back to Iowa?"

"Soon as I can save enough gold."

"You even remember Iowa? Your hometown? What your house looked like? Your family? If you were going home, you'd have left already."

"I think about home every day," Jules said, which was true. "I remember it like it was yesterday." That was a lie. He remembered that his house was white and that it had been surrounded by fields of wheat. He remembered a red bicycle and a green tractor. He remembered potato dinners with his family, vacations to a lake cabin in Minnesota, and a drive-in movie theater where he made out with his high school girlfriend. But he couldn't picture his parents' smiles, or how they'd spent the time at that cabin, or the name of the girlfriend.

"You've helped us in the past," Chase said. "I won't forget that. I'll give you the same deal you gave us: goods for gold."

"This is a girl's life you're bartering."

"It's a better offer than Barning made when my son disappeared."

Jules winced. He hadn't realized one of the kids had been Chase's. Had Bethany known? Jules felt around his pockets for gold. There were several pieces in his pocket. Some gold coins, a dozen fillings, a wedding band. But he hesitated a moment. This wasn't their usual protocol. Chuck and Jules found things for money. They didn't spend their own money. Would Sarah reimburse him? She probably didn't have a cent to her name. Jules suddenly felt ashamed of himself for thinking that. But how much money had he and Chuck made? They had made people's birthdays, helped defend the town, kept stomachs full in lean times, and saved lives. But they had done it all for money. He thought about going home to Iowa. How much more gold did he need before he could go? He always said *more* but never *how much*.

Jules held four gold coins out to Chase.

Chase looked skeptically at the coins for a moment before he put them in his pocket. "There's this group," Chase began. "Some call them marauders. They're more like nomads. In the winter, they hole up in some caves bootleggers used to use. In the summer, they live on an old pumpkin farm."

"Pumpkins?"

"Used to give hayrides. Pumpkin painting for kids, hard cider for adults. They still grow pumpkins, but it's not someplace you'd want to take your kids. About two miles down Route Seventeen."

Jules wanted to tell him that he was going to go back to Iowa someday. He wanted to say that Chase was jaded, that there was still room for decency. "I'm sorry about your son."

Chase nodded, though he looked surprised by the condolence. Jules climbed his horse and galloped back to Chuck.

"Old Pumpkin farm on Route Seventeen. Know the place?"

"Sure," Chuck said. "He told you? Just like that?"

They wheeled their horses around and started down the road. "Sure, after I gave him some gold."

"You didn't," Chuck said. Jules could hear the smile in his voice.

"It was stupid," Jules said, shaking his head. "This girl is dead. I can feel it in my bones."

"Don't give me that. Why are you so sure she's dead?"

"Why are you sure she isn't?"

Chuck shrugged. "So why did you give that asshole your gold? *Money in, never out.* That's our motto." Jules rolled his eyes. "It was the right thing to do." He spurred Molly and galloped ahead before he had to endure Chuck's self-righteous reaction.

They stopped that night in an old orchard that was more pines than apple trees now. They picked some McIntoshes and cooked them over a fire until the skins split. A clear night, they slept under wool blankets, dozing beneath the stars, the promise of cooler days ahead in a northern breeze.

That night, Jules dreamt of home again. Golden fields, a coming thunderstorm, the smell of smoke. He turned around but saw no fire. He brushed his fingertips over the tops of the wheat, but when he did, the plants turned to ash. Slowly, starting from one end of the field and rolling along like a wave, the yellow stalks disintegrated, blowing away like so much dust. Jules ran through the field, trying to outpace it. He tripped and landed in a mound of dirt. Looking around, he saw that nothing grew around him. Everything was dead. He looked at his hands and saw black, mummified flesh.

Jules woke, his hair matted to his forehead with sweat.

After another six hours of riding, Chuck said they were getting close. They pulled off the side of the road and, getting down from the horses, led them by their reins up a hillside. Chuck and Jules found a game trail and followed it, the hill growing steeper, jagged rocks piercing through pine needles and decomposing leaves.

When they reached a summit, they tied their horses to a spruce and found a clearing that overlooked a farm. Chuck carried binoculars, and, sure enough, he spotted fields thick with pumpkins. He also spotted movement near a barn and what had once been a visitor's center. It was too far to make out any particular face, but they decided to sit and wait. If there were captives, maybe he and Chuck would be able to see where they were held. That was the plan, until they got caught.

Jules heard the dry rustle of dead leaves behind them, but before he could turn around, he heard the metallic click of a gun's hammer.

"Drop your pistol belts," said a man's voice, gruff and baritone. The voice of someone who wasn't fucking around. Jules loosened his leather belt and it slid to his ankles with a muffled *thump*. Something hit him on the back of the head, and he fell to his hands and knees. His vision flashed then darkened. Clutching his skull and groaning, Jules turned and saw Chuck on the ground too, knocked out cold. Before he could turn and get a look at their attackers, a hood slipped over his head. His hands and ankles were then tied. Jules tried to resist, and that was when a second thump on the head knocked him out.

When Jules woke, the sun was setting. He found himself sitting, his arms tied to the trunk of an oak tree. A half dozen men circled a bonfire a few yards away, their backs to him. Beyond the men stood the barn and the farmhouse that he and Chuck had seen from the ridgeline. His head pounded, and his eyes ached. Jules squirmed, trying to pull his arms free, but the rope dug into his wrists. Was there a jagged rock he could use to cut the rope? Only tree roots snaked above the yellowed grass.

Someone coughed. When Jules turned his head, he saw Chuck tied to an adjacent tree. Blood ran down Chuck's forehead and into his eyes. Apparently hearing the cough, the men at the fire turned around and approached them.

One of the men took the lead. He had a large belly, bald head, and gray beard. His watery eyes bugged out of his head. He looked like a down-on-his-luck high school janitor. "Anyone know you're here?"

"No," Jules said. "Just us."

The janitor took a bite from an apple. "You scouting to rob us?"

"We're looking for a girl," Chuck said.

"Ain't we all?" one of the men said, and the others laughed.

Jules counted seven total. "She was taken," he said. "Few nights back. Sister's looking for her. Name's Clare."

The men had all seemed amused, but at the mention of Clare, their smirks vanished. They exchanged glances.

"Clare, huh?" the janitor said. "Lady in distress. And what, you two are the cavalry?"

"Do you have her?" Chuck asked. He was using his tough-guy voice, but it cracked on the last word, sounding more hopeful than intimidating.

The janitor turned around. He nodded at someone, and they walked over to the farmhouse. A moment later, someone left the farmhouse and walked toward them. They wore an old, gray sweatshirt, the hood drawn. When they neared, Jules saw that it was a woman. Brown hair, blue eyes. She stood a few feet away. When she lowered the sweatshirt's hood, Jules saw the crescent-shaped scar on her forehead. It was Clare. Smoke drifted from a cigarette clenched in her lips. A scoped hunting rifle was slung over her shoulder.

"What's this about?" she asked.

"These guys are here to rescue you," the janitor said and laughed.

Clare blew out a pair of smoke rings, but the wind soon took them away. "Sarah?" she asked, and the janitor nodded. Clare shook her head, clearly annoyed. "What are you going to do with them?"

"Kill them," someone said.

Jules couldn't explain why, but he was certain Sarah had known this particular twist. *I'm going to fucking kill her.*

"Don't be an asshole," someone else said. "Let's ransom them."

"Where you boys from?" the janitor asked.

"Barning," Jules said. Getting ransomed back to Barning didn't sound so bad. After everything they had done for the town, it was the least its citizens could do. Would they pay what these guys wanted, though? Jules weighed the pros and cons of vomiting.

A few more people called out ideas. The group seemed divided between Team Ransom and Team Kill. A minority suggested eating them. It wasn't a particularly lively debate, however. No one seemed passionate one way or another. Ultimately, they lost interest and gathered again around the fire.

"If you let us go, we can help you," Jules said. "We find things for a living. Anything you want, we can get it."

The janitor yawned and shrugged. He tossed an apple core to the ground. "We'll sleep on it and get back to you tomorrow."

He went to the farmhouse, and Chuck and Jules were alone again. "We need to get the fuck out of here," Jules said.

Chuck nodded. "Thoughts?"

Someone near the fire laughed. One by one, the men went into the farmhouse for the night until only one remained. He tossed the occasional log on the fire and sometimes glanced over his shoulder at the prisoners.

Jules pulled on the ropes tying his wrists until the skin was raw and bloody. His elbows and shoulders ached, and his brain felt too large for his skull. He thought that he might be able to fray the rope by rubbing it against the coarse bark, but it became clear his wrists would give out before the rope did. At some point, he drifted to sleep.

Jules woke to someone's hand over his mouth. His eyes shot open, and he saw Clare crouched in front of him, her face a foot from his. A hooked hunting knife glinted in her hand, and Jules pressed himself against the tree. There was nowhere to go.

"Don't make a sound," she whispered.

He breathed hard into her palm. Clare's hand was rough and smelled like onions and gun oil. Slowly, she took her hand from his mouth and reached for his wrists. She slid the blade under the rope, and, with a single motion, sliced through it. When the tension gave out, Jules clenched his shoulders and leaned forward. He felt like he hadn't taken a full breath in eight hours. Jules removed the remaining rope from his wrists, the yellow braids dyed red with blood.

As Clare cut Chuck free, Jules turned to look at the fire. The guard was still there, hunched over in a chair. The fire had burned down to embers, a single yellow flame still licking the edges of a log. He heard the faint sound of snoring.

On all fours, his rope still tied to his wrists, Chuck crept over to Jules.

"Our packs and weapons?" Jules whispered.

Clare shook her head.

"The horses?" Jules thought of Molly. Would they eat her? As much as he didn't like riding horses, she didn't deserve that.

"Can't," Clare whispered back. "You need to go on foot."

Chuck frowned. "Fuck. Okay, we got to leave now, then. Get a lead on them before they notice we're gone."

"I'm not going," Clare said. "This is where I belong."

"Are you fucking with us?" Chuck asked.

"You can't want to stay here," Jules said. "With those guys?"

"They're not bad," she said. "They're protective of their own. Got to be." She tilted her head at them and snorted. "Look at you two. You got a home in Barning. A roof over your head. You never had to live on the road. Never sleeping in the same place for more than a week. These people are my home."

"Your sister sent us," Jules said. He looked over at the man slumped near the fire. Was he asleep? Had Clare drugged him somehow? "Sarah's your home."

Clare shook her head. "That's all Sarah ever talks about. Our home burned. We watched some men kill our parents while we hid in a treehouse. Sarah lost her mind. Doesn't remember or won't. Thinks we just need to go back, and it'll all be there again."

"She loves you," Jules said.

Clare winced. "The sister she loves...I'm not that person anymore." Clare reached behind her neck and unclasped a chain. A laminated peacock feather hung from it, traced in silver. She coiled the chain in her hand and gave it to Jules.

"What should we tell Sarah?" Jules asked.

"Whatever you want." Clare turned and crept back to the farmhouse.

The fire was mostly embers now, but somewhere in there a log popped. Jules and Chuck ran downhill, through the pumpkin patches, and to the road, headed back toward Barning.

It took a week to walk back. Jules and Chuck foraged for early, sour apples and found patches of squashberries that had not yet rotted off the bush. Searching rusted cars that resembled ancient carapaces of long-dead insects, they found some empty plastic bottles that they filled along roadside streams. For the most part, they walked in silence. The murderous heat yielded to overcast skies. A chill sneaked into the night air, and it lingered longer each morning.

If their captors pursued them, they didn't know about it. The roads were desolate. The harvest had begun, and most travel had ceased until the snow melted in April.

"The hell are we going to tell Sarah?" Chuck asked when they were nearly home.

"The truth," Jules said.

Chuck spit out a sunflower seed. "She deserves better than the truth."

"You can tell her, then." Jules picked at an apple peel stuck between his teeth. "I'm getting a beer and one of Lucy's steaks."

"No, boss," Chuck said. "This one's yours. You're calling the shots, remember?"

"I thought you had a thing for Sarah?"

"Better to stick with Barning chicks," Chuck replied.

Jules shook his head. "Didn't you like that she wasn't from these parts?"

Chuck shrugged and went to the ranch to get a few copper pieces for the tavern. Jules went to Bobby's Place to find Sarah.

Sarah was on the porch, waiting for him. He imagined she had stood watch there every night since they'd left two weeks ago. When she saw Jules, she stood. Steam rose from a cup of tea in her hand. "Where's my sister?" she asked.

Jules walked up the steps. "We found her."

"Where is she?" Sarah was cleaner than the last time he'd seen her, though she still wore the same rags. Her cheeks looked a bit fuller. Town life agreed with her.

Jules patted his pockets until he found the necklace. He pulled it out and gave it to her.

"This is hers. Where is she?" Sarah's lip trembled.

"She..." Jules smelled a wheat field. He'd never thought that growing wheat had a smell, but as he caught that strange scent, it brought him back to his childhood. As soon as he noticed it, it was gone.

Sarah clasped the necklace in her palm. "Jules, where is she?"

"She's dead. I'm sorry, Sarah."

She cried and Jules put his hand on her shoulder. Even as he was doing it, however, the gesture seemed wholly inadequate. Her parents had been murdered. Her home had burned down. And now her sister was gone. There wasn't a thing he could do to change that.

Sarah put her hands on the porch railing and leaned her weight on it. "Oh my god," she said between sobs. "No one. I have no one now. And there's no good people left anywhere."

Jules tried to respond, to tell her she was wrong. He took a drag from his cigarette and felt a sudden and inexplicably warm breeze before the autumn chill returned.

"No," Sarah said angrily. She turned to look at him, her eyes red and watery. "The good people didn't live."

That night, Jules lay awake in his bed. His back ached from too many nights of sleeping on the ground. The mattress felt good, but he tossed and turned. He tried to think of Iowa, wanted to dream about it, about the wheat fields and his red bicycle, but the memory eluded him. When he finally did go to sleep, he dreamed of a house, but not the one where he grew up.

Jules dreamed of the barn Chuck was trying to sell him. He dreamed that it had a wood stove, that he was starting a fire, blowing on the embers to stoke the flames. Smoke got in his eyes and nose, but it was a good smell. There was someone else there. A woman? He didn't recognize her face, but she was beautiful. She sat on a green couch and read a book. The feeling of contentedness was so intoxicating that it startled him awake.

Jules sat up in his bed and looked around his room, trying to recognize it as his own. Eventually, he grabbed the dented coffee can that contained his life's savings, hidden in a suitcase in his closet, and went downstairs where Chuck was making dandelion root tea.

"I'm ready to buy the barn," Jules said.

Jules found Sarah sitting in a folding chair on the porch, eating eggs and beans from a tin plate. She looked away when Jules approached.

"Morning," he said.

She pretended not to hear him.

He took a seat on a chair next to her and put the house keys on her plate beside a runny egg.

"What's this?" she asked.

"The keys to your new house."

"What?"

"The barn house that Chuck's fixing up." Jules nodded at it across the street. "It's yours now. I just bought it."

"I don't understand."

"I'm leaving town, but I think you should stay. Barning's a good place. Folks here are decent. I think you should stick around. Maybe see if you can get a job at the tavern. Get married. Raise a family. Whatever you want. Shit, you can even sell the house and keep the money. Up to you."

"If it's such a nice place, why are you leaving?"

Jules looked at the fields in mid-harvest and potholed road he had walked along for the past twenty years. A column of smoke rose from the woodstove at the ranch.

"Because I have a home," he said. "But it's not here."

"What do you want from me?" she asked.

Jules shrugged. He tried to say *nothing* but couldn't bring himself to. If he wanted something from her, it wasn't something he could articulate.

Jules got up and stretched. He had a long way to go, and he wanted to get started. Before he left, he turned to look at Sarah one last time. "Take care of yourself."

Within an hour, Jules had everything packed. Considering his job was to find things for people, he had surprisingly few possessions of his own. He loaded up the saddlebags on his ten-speed. He hitched up a small trailer, one that had once been used to carry a toddler. Now it held fifty pounds of wheat, dozens of jars of tomatoes and chicken, a few boxes of ammunition, five gallons of water, a cast iron skillet and two backpacks of clothes. There were two atlases of America's highways and a hardcover of *The Old Man and The Sea*. He carried a .22 rifle slung over his back and a handgun tucked into his jeans.

Chuck knelt beside the bike, rubbing sunflower seed oil on the chain. "This place won't be right without you." Chuck had the same fake smile he had used a lifetime ago when he had to explain how he got a D in Psych 100 to his parents. It made Jules feel young again, or at least like a young man with thinning hair and the beginnings of osteoarthritis.

"You won't even notice I'm gone."

Chuck stood up and dusted off his knees. "It's not true." He held out his hand.

Jules shook his hand and looked away, blinking quickly. Chuck pulled him in for a long hug and took off Jules' Lake Monster baseball cap. He replaced it with his own handmade leather cowboy hat.

Some of the townsfolk lined up outside like a choir, waiting their turn to say goodbye. There were teary-eyed *good lucks* and joking *see you soons*.

Jules got onto the bicycle and began to peddle, tilting his new cowboy hat to block out the sun. It was a long ride. Best as he could tell with the old atlas, Barning, Vermont, to Red Oak, Iowa, was one thousand four hundred and twenty-six miles. With some luck and good weather, he could make it before November.

A memory suddenly came to him. It was late fall. He could see his father standing in the driveway of their house. He wore a greasy sleeveless shirt and a bandana. Jules had just learned to ride his red bicycle without the training wheels, and now he was going to go meet up with his friends to play baseball.

His dad waved a meaty hand, stained with grease from the tractor, and called to him: "Come home before it gets dark."

Jules smiled, his teeth rattling as the bike bumped along the rutted road. He was going home.

Dehydrated

Chloe Viner

I imagine myself
living in the water
in a cubbyhole between
bubbles and seaweed
rain takes me to the treetops
shooting downward I find
myself
weeping out of a willow
but my feet are in
brown dirt and gravel
in springtime, in wintertime,
orange days, black days,
days where the sun seems to never set
days where the blisters bleed into my tracks
I'm just another wounded
animal being hunted
I feel hope when it rains
running down my
cheekbones.

Whitey and the Kid

Karen Marie Menzel

for Melissa Wubben, Oak Creek Farm

My day started normal enough. Well, what passes for normal these days. Fed the animals, cleaned up. Sat at the breakfast table staring out the window, held down by weighty memories. Concave triangles of soot darken the window corners—leftovers from The Burn even though it's been a couple decades. Grey drifts slowly collect on win-dowsills, worse than gravel dust. I don't know where it all comes from. Barning, VT, might be the "Oasis of the Collapse," but ash and dust still killed our crops.

"Ecology doesn't care how special we are," Chuck used to say. It's been six months since cancer took him, and I hear his voice as I scrape the remains of my goat-milk omelet into the scraps bucket. Unlike planet Earth, I'm sliding into my old age disconnected from the rest. The sun still shines through the haze, but each day is just a little less bright. This is life now when I'm not with the animals. Grey and dull. I know Chuck wanted me to "keep hope alive" after, but it's harder without him now than surviving the Collapse together. Apocalypse is easier with a partner, I guess. Especially a survivalist eighth-generation farmer and genuine Vermont Woodchuck.

Mouse's deep bark jolts me out of my woolgathering. He gets the other dogs going. It's too damn early for that racket. God, I miss coffee.

Why couldn't Vermont have been the coffee bean capital of North America? Vermont's famous dairy cows died, but feral hogs are everywhere. I never thought I'd get tired of bacon and maple syrup over acorn-flour and cornmeal pancakes, but it turns out there is a limit. Thank God the hens are still laying and indoor potted cherry tomatoes and onions won't quit. They're tougher than either of us. Probably still be here after we're gone. After I'm gone.

I shrug on a flannel, shove my feet into wellies, and holler at the dogs to pipe down, but I've still got my Collapse instincts. *Excalibur* is an ancient but sharp pitchfork I keep by the door, the wood handle polished from use. There's a tone to Mouse's bark I don't like. Intruder. Best to be ready. I take the back way around the house.

Fog is thick on the ground in the valley, and our yard is white with mist. I move through the garden softly, making my way around great grandma's iron-handled well pump. The old well with the squeaky windmill keeps the house, barn, and irrigation system supplied with running water. Without it, I wouldn't be able to water the animals and keep the garden going. I don't know what kind of rock is under the farm, but whatever it is keeps the local aquifer clean. Maybe that's why Barning's an oasis. Some trick of fate left us clean water.

Mouse and Mister bark their heads off, wild to get at something on the garage's flat roof, their dark shapes displacing the swirling fog. As I come closer, pitchfork lowered and ready, a hunched form is visible on top of the small building.

"Shut it," I holler at the dogs. "Back." I get a whine of protest out of Mister, but both cattle dogs jump away from the whatever-it-is and run to me, then past me, around back to the wall, yipping in disobedience brought on by over-excitement. I haven't been exercising them enough since losing Chuck.

The shape lifts its head. It's a small person. A kid.

"Mouse," I say in my most commanding tone, then back it up with my get-over-here-right-now whistle. Mouse yelps and then slinks back to my side, Mister right behind him.

"Doc, you gotta help," the kid says. "Down the crossing. Please." The kid stands up as the words tumble out of her, apparently not bothered in the least by the fact that she's still on the garage roof.

I don't see any injuries. Well, no blood anyway. She's wearing what most of the village kids wear—whatever they can find. In this case, it's a much mended and stained t-shirt and sweatpants. No shoes, hair cut short in the careless sort of way a parent with too much to do might manage for a child who won't hold still. Her face is streaked with dirt. Tears maybe.

"Who's down crossing way?" I ask. All the villagers call me Doc, especially when they want something, even though I'm only a veterinarian. Either way, useful skills, and these days you make do with whoever you've got.

"Bunch of kids," she says. "Come quick." And just like that she leaps from the garage and scampers down the walnut tree, tearing off down the dirt road.

Mouse and Mister perk up their ears, look at her, look back at me.

"Oh alright." I sigh. Both dogs leap after the kid, clods of dirt flying up behind them as they dig in. "Mud season..." I duck into the garage, grab a first aid kit, then squelch down the dirt road as fast I can in a pair of wellies. Fortunately, the crossing isn't too far.

I hear the kids long before I can see them. Yelling, laughing. They don't sound like they're in distress.

I scowl. A peaceful morning disturbed for nothing.

Then I hear one of the dogs yelp. It's not a "you're playing too hard" yelp. It's an "ouch, that really hurt" yelp. Then I'm up over the curve of the hill and I can see what's going on.

There's a knot of scruffy boys on my side of the bridge. They're clustered around the base of a tree, throwing rocks at Mouse and Mister and the girl. Most of the rocks are off target, but one hits the girl right in the chest. It must have hurt like hell, but she isn't fazed. She nails the perpetrator in the head with a rock of her own. He doesn't go down, but he ducks and covers. Mouse and Mister are barking and running around and nobody's noticed me yet.

I've still got *Excalibur*. And my llama whistle. It's actually a goose call, but you blow on it just right and it sounds like a llama in danger. It's a horrible sound, and if you haven't heard it, go startle a llama if you can find one. No. Don't do that. Llamas are not like other "prey" animals. They are fierce, territorial, and protect anything they consider theirs. Like the farm. Like me and Mouse and Mister.

Kuzco and Pacha's grazing meadow borders the river. It won't take them long to get to the bridge. I raise my pitchfork over my head and shake it, blowing on the llama whistle. A god-awful racket rises above the yelling kids and barking dogs. Mouse and Mister peel off and come running back to me, leaving the girl alone in the middle of the road, but the noise I'm making is sufficient distraction, so the boys don't keep clobbering her.

Everyone stares at the old woman waving her pitchfork, blowing her goose call. The boys look at me and at the rocks in their hands and at each other.

I brace myself.

Then two angry black llamas crest the ridge and charge past me. Wagner's "Ride of the Valkyries" plays in my head. The boys break ranks and scatter, beelining back to the village side of the bridge.

Kuzco and Pacha run back and forth, chasing off the stragglers. Mouse and Mister are smart enough to stay out of their way. The girl darts over to the tree the boys had first surrounded and climbs up, out of the llamas' reach. It takes me a while to calm all four animals and make my way to the tree.

"You okay, kid?" I see her curled around a branch, shaking with sobs.

"They hurt him," she says, snot running over her lip. "Whitey's hurt."

My eyes track down to a grey-brown bundle wedged between branch and trunk, splashed red with blood. It's not moving. The stillness of death.

"Pass him down, kid." I say gently. Poor child—this is probably her first dead cat. I'll have to tell the sheriff about the boys and the attack. Cruelty to animals is a sign of worse to come, and with everything we've lived through so far, I'm not about to sink back down into that chaos again. I'd label it a return to animalistic natures, but no animal's ever been as intently evil as mankind.

This cat is like us, I think. We've lived through hell and we're dying one by one, beaten. Sniffling but trying to be grown up about it, the kid masters herself and passes down the bedraggled corpse. I gather it up gently and...

Oh. Oh lord. It's not a cat.

The kid slides down the trunk and wipes her nose on her forearm. Kuzco trots over, but the dogs aren't reacting like the kid's a threat, so he and Pacha leave her alone.

I carefully lay the limp opossum on the ground and kneel, checking its wounds. Its eyes stare—open and glassy. It's battered and bruised. The blood is from a torn ear. And even though it stinks to high heaven, I lean until my ear rests against its small body. It looks dead, but, well, "playing opossum" isn't just a saying.

"He's dead, isn't he?" The kid watches, tears continuing to fall, looking at death. Things around here have been pretty calm the last few years and she's young. Maybe this is her first experience with this kind of loss?

It's faint, but I hear a heartbeat and shallow breathing inside the small animal's chest. I sit up, and I'm puzzled why smiling hurts. Guess I haven't used those muscles for a long time.

"Nope. What'd you say his name is? Whitey? Whitey is alive."

The kid's dark eyes glare at me dubiously. I guess she's had adults lie to her before.

"Whitey is an opossum. They don't move very fast, so when they are threatened or get really scared, their bodies sort of... shut down. This tricks the attacker into leaving them alone, thinking they are already dead."

The kid listens to me carefully, and I watch her slowly give in to hope.

I take advantage of Whitey's temporary paralysis to treat his...uh, *her* injuries. Whitey is female. The kid watches everything I'm doing as if she's memorizing proper opossum care. While I'm at it, I give her a lesson on marsupials and show her Whitey's pouch. She already knows about the prehensile tail.

"I found him, I mean her, when she was just a little baby," she tells me. "I fed her all by myself. She likes to ride on my shoulders."

Food was scarce in the village sometimes—I bet it was hard on the kid to share her food. Probably her parents didn't approve of it either. "Did your parents let you keep him inside?" People did, on occasion, eat opossum, and I was curious how Whitey had made it to adulthood.

"I don't have any." The kid says it matter of fact, without emotion. Ah. One of the pastor's orphans, then. I'd been to the church to treat them on occasion. I vaguely remembered a kid who could have been this one, but I definitely didn't remember an opossum. Opossums didn't live very long, though, and I hadn't been to the village for a year. Too busy taking care of Chuck—and mourning him. The raising of Whitey probably happened while I was away.

For the first time in months, thinking about Chuck didn't suck me under. I was still sad, but it didn't take me over.

"Well," I say, getting slowly to my feet, making sure I don't tweak my trick knee. "Let's get her somewhere safe to recover, yeah?"

The kid looks at me then back at the village. The church has been lost in the fog. The town looks quiet, but the fog hides those boys. I don't have high expectations of Whitey being long for this world if the kid goes back into town.

"Okay," the kid says, carefully picking up the limp opossum. Then she starts walking back to the farm. Mouse and Mister escort her, running ahead and then back, as if she's a miniature me. Kuzko and Pacha nose me for treats, but finding me empty-handed, they snort indignantly and go back to their meadow.

I make a mental note to give each of them something special after I get Whitey and the kid settled. Normal is going to look different now. I'm smart enough to realize that Mouse is happier with Mister and Kuzco is happier with Pacha. I lost my Woodchuck, but I don't have to stay alone. The whole world's been paralyzed, heartbeat slow, breathing shallow, hoping the predators don't see us. Shut down. Me most of all, since Chuck died. There's a time to stop playing opossum.

The kid walks with purpose and confidence down the road. She doesn't remember a "before" when electricity worked. There's never been refrigerators or ambulances in her world. An antique train buff will get the steam-powered locomotive going again and change everything. It's the nature of human beings to evolve, face challenges, improve the human condition. Yes, those village boys were cruel. But there's also a preacher who takes in orphans, a kid who adopts an orphaned opossum, an old veterinarian who had just about given up considering taking on an apprentice.

I pick up *Excalibur*, squelch through the mud, and let myself slowly give in to hope.

Always Too Much and Never Enough

Chloe Viner

They get mad at me
for smiling
it's inappropriate in
such times
also
I need to smile
more
for to be a woman
is to always be too much
or not enough
like an avocado
my window for being
perfect is ephemeral
I never seem to
time it right

A lion's mane makes him
suffer in the heat at all times
but he can still
be
free

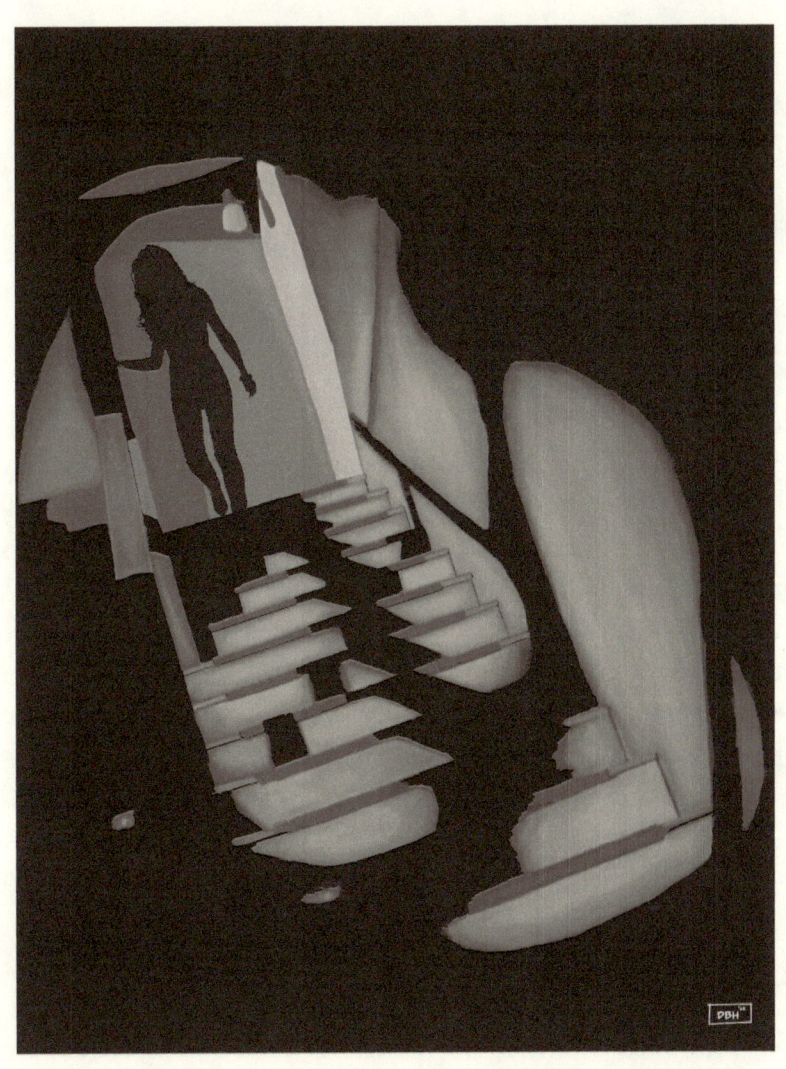

Doom Saloon

Renee S. DeCamillis

The rusty chains of the *Bar Closed* sign creak and clatter from the howling winds outside the Silver Blade Saloon. The bloated moon's silvery sheen sends out an army of towering shadows throughout the small walled-in town of Barning, Vermont, where keeping human monsters out is as important as eliminating inhuman monsters from within. It's that time of night, or rather morning, when not a single soul should be sitting at any of Lucy's bar stools. Only those free of the heavy burden of a soul come 'round the bar near The Devil's Hour—an occurrence happening with much more frequency lately.

But then there are always the town drunks, of which Barning has many.

Lucy strolls out of the swinging batwing doors of the bar's backroom as nonchalantly as she can fake. Her scuffed-up leather engineer boots clomp against the plank-board floor with every heavy step she takes. A smile plastered on her deceptively youthful face, she wipes ashes off her bustier before anyone notices. As she sets down a bucket of warm soapy water onto the counter, she throws a curious glance toward the back where she left Zeppie behind to clean up the remnants of the battle from earlier. With the rapid beating of her heart, she hopes nothing else ventures out of the tunnels in the wine cellar before she can finally clear the bar of its last patrons. Dave and Jerry, both laughing obnoxiously loud, still remain sitting at the bar, refusing to adhere to

Lucy's rollback on last call. Their Mason jar mugs have sat empty for almost an hour.

Where the hell is Zeke?! She looks over the heads of the crimson-faced duo, searching for her other bouncer. He didn't show up out back to help with the surprise attack, and now he still hasn't shown his face to help with the drunks.

When you want something done and done right...

Lucy adjusts the silver dagger hanging from her leather belt and resting against her curvy hip as she glances at the cuckoo clock behind the bar.

2:30.

As The Devil's Hour creeps closer, Lucy's senses kick into high gear. A prickly sensation at the base of her neck and a knot in her stomach, ringing in her ears.

Something else is coming. Time to clean fucking house!

"Not that I don't like the eye candy and the titillating conversation, boys." Lucy throws the drunks a wink and a smile before continuing. "But I need to close up shop and get my beauty sleep." She tosses her long sable locks over her shoulder and strategically adjusts her bustier, making sure her movements cause a glint of the silver blade to shimmer in the lantern light.

Every person in Barning knows Lucy's way with blades. Not even one of them has been able to beat her in the weekly knife throwing competitions out back of the bar.

"Them there bootiful blues shine brighter dan dat blade ever could, Mizz Luzy." Dave's words slur out as drops of his spittle sprinkle onto the rustic oak bar.

With one swift and graceful movement, she pulls the blade from her belt, swings it in an arc over her head with a flourish, and drives the tip into the top of the bar beside their empty mugs. "Well, looks like you've gone and made Sparkles here a bit jealous." With a furrowed brow, she leans her right ear down close to the blade, listens for a moment. "Yep, just as I suspected. She calls a challenge." Lucy yanks the blade out of the hard wood and twirls it in her hand, then stops a brief second to check her reflection and fluff her hair. Her intense eyes peer past the silver blade, straight at Dave. "You up for a challenge out back here this weekend, ol' Davey Boy? You know she wants a piece of you now, right?" A mischievous smile spreads wide. The flickering flames of the bar-top lanterns make her ruby-berried lips shine.

With sudden shock painted on his ruddy face, Dave falters in his seat and falls off the side of the bar stool.

Jerry clumsily slides off his stool, crouches to help his inebriated buddy up off the floor. After tossing a pouch of veggie seeds and a bundle of lavender on the bar to pay their bill, he tugs Dave toward the front door. "Don't worry. I'll get this ol' drunk out of here for ya, Luce. No worries. Sorry to be a bother."

"Oh, no bother," she says as she hooks her silver dagger back onto her belt. "I enjoy the company, just not *this* late." She reaches toward the bucket, grabs a cloth out of the warm soapy water, and starts wiping down the bar. "Last call's at two, boys. Don't forget, or I'll have to send my flying monkeys after you both." She waves with her free hand. "See you tomorrow night, guys."

Staying open until 3:00 AM, like back in the early days, started posing a threat once the monstrosities began coming through those tunnels under the bar. Tonight's attack happened much earlier than normal. Lucy and her partners, Double Z, can manage more frequent attacks, but if the creatures also start emerging earlier each time—now that won't do well for business. And this is not the first time this has happened.

As Dave and Jerry stumble out the front doors and onto the porch, Zeke pops into view. He leans against the outside doorframe, a joint poking out from under his shaggy shoulder-length dreaded hair and over his ear, another one hanging out the corner of his lips. When the lingerers pass by, he stands tall and puffs out his burly chest as smoke blows out of his mouth.

Pinched between thumb and pointer, he pulls out the joint. "Be ca'eful out the'e, fellas. Betta get on home befo'e ya wives come huntin' ya down."

Laughter and grunts, the only replies heard. A blink later, towering shadows of the night swallow the two town drunks, and all grows eerily quiet. No more titters. No more talking. Not even the sound of their shuffling footfalls. The skeleton-white orb in the sky looms over Barning.

Zeke pops the joint back between his lips, turns heel, and strolls inside. He shuts and locks the doors behind him, heads toward Lucy. Just as he steps up to the front of the bar, a crash and clatter sound out from the dark side of the barroom.

They both spin toward the shadows of the closed-off section under the loft on the left.

Neither of them says a word. Experience leads their actions.

Lucy's blade replaces the cloth in her hand before she even knows what caused the ruckus. Zeke's joint hangs from the corner of his lips like a cigarette as he pulls his revolver out from the waist of his jeans behind his back. They both step away from the bar and head toward the sound, communicating only with their eyes and head movements.

As they edge their way closer to the darkness under the loft, they hear scratching and clawing on the wood-plank floor under the tables. Lucy's foot is about to step into the shadows when out runs a growl-hissing raccoon baring its sharp teeth. Its quick, defensive movements knock down a hanging chair from one of the tables, which tumbles over next to another overturned chair on the floor—the obvious origin of the crashing noise a moment ago. A reflexive sidestep-jump moves Lucy out of the night prowler's way, knocking Zeke out of the way as well. It's not her first run-in with the local wildlife desperately searching for food.

Brow beaded in sweat, Zeke throws out his arm, gun cocked and aimed at the furry little trickster.

Lucy bats his hand aside. "No way, man! No shooting coons. They're harmless creatures of the night. It just wants food. Save the holy silver bullets for the real threats that lurk in the dark."

The masked intruder scurry-waddles past them, making dragging sounds across the barroom floor and under the double doors of the back room.

Zeke uncocks the hammer, drops his arm to his side. With his free hand, he wipes the sweat from his forehead. "Luce, don't you think it's time to seal up those tunnels and keep the demonic riffraff out of our town?"

She turns away, starts heading back across the barroom. "They'll just find another way in, Zeke. They always do. Just like the raiders." Her silver blade twirls in her hand, then flies up over her head, flipping end-over-end. She catches it by the hilt on its descent. Tricks she does when tensions run high. "Haven't you figured it out yet? Walls create only an illusion of protection."

"Yeah, but..." He pauses, leans down toward one of the only candles still burning on a nearby table, relights his joint, continues in a strained voice. "At least then it might be a bit mo'e of a struggle fo' them. With that tunnel entrance wide open, and *all* its serpentine offshoots, it's like we're *welcomin'* them in." A few smoke rings puff out of his mouth along with a nervous titter. "At the rate we're goin', might as well re-name this place *Doom Saloon*."

Lucy cocks her head. "Huh...Clutch...Man, I wish we had tunes like theirs now. But, *hell* no, dude. Stop dwelling on the negative."

Another toke. More smoke rings. "It's been twenty yea's since The Collapse, Luce. I think it's safe to say, ya family isn't..."

The silver blade flies past his Medusa-like snaky dreads, straight through the last smoke ring hovering in the air, stabbing into the support beam behind his head.

"Bite your tongue," Lucy says.

He leans back and glances over his shoulder at the sheen of the silver blade sticking out of the oak pillar, reflecting his startled expression back at him. So close, he could stick out his tongue and lick it.

Ever since The Collapse, following the freakish solar flares that flipped the old ways of the world into chaos and darkness, Lucy's held out hope to find someone from her family who may have survived. Numerous explosions and wildfires decimated much of the land in the early aftermath of the flares. Next came the raiding murder-mobs that swept across the country, which led to more fires—just because they could. The smell of burning flesh still haunts her wakeful nightmares.

Maybe her family hid away in time and survived like her and Double Z. Maybe in the wine cellar or one of the underground tunnels under the bar.

It's been twenty long years.

Before then, Lucy fled every request her Mama and Nonna had thrown her way for her to bring her green thumb back to Vermont to work the family business alongside them. Vacca's Vineyards was quite the rave back in the day. Wine tasting events for Sunday brunch at the bar always packed the place. Such a hit with all the tourists as well as the locals. Bonfire Fridays and Saturdays in Spring and Summer and Fall—extra-large on each equinox and solstice—and twinkle lights hung all around the yard. Patrons and friends strolled from colorful Adirondack chairs around the fire to the dance floor inside the saloon-style bar, the flung-open barn doors in the back spread wide like open arms, welcoming everyone in for a hug.

In addition to Vacca's highly sought-after wines, whiskey was also a favorite among patrons, though Lucy never knew where the supply came from. Somehow the barrel in the wine cellar always remained full, like Nonna's always fully stocked cookie jar when Lucy was a little girl.

Anytime Lucy asked about that whisky barrel, her mother would just brush Lucy's long hair out of her face, tuck it behind her ear, and say, "Don't you worry your pretty little head about that, Lucy-loo. Mama and Nonna—we have our ways." She would always follow that up by singing "You are My Sunshine," the song she'd sung ever since Lucy was a baby.

Investing her future in the family business was not for free-strutting Lucy back then. She took her college education and her green thumb a little further east to forge her own path, free from family judgment and squabbles among cousins and siblings and aunts and uncles and everyone, where the loudest person was always deemed the one who knew best, the one whose advice you should follow—no questions asked.

Lucy always questions.

"Where were *you* hiding earlier?" Lucy grabs the cleaning cloth off the bar, tosses it back into the bucket of soapy water. Suds slop over the edge. "You *obviously* weren't helping to get the drunks outta here while Zeppie and I had a run-in with an early arrival from the tunnels."

Zeke tucks his gun back into the waist of his jeans and pulls Lucy's blade out of the support beam beside his head. "Shit, Luce! Anotha one showed up early? I had no idea." He shakes his head. "Man, that shit's happenin' a lot mo'e lately." He walks up to the bar and sets the silver blade in front of her. "I was just calming myself down with a little toke on the po'ch befo'e coming back in to deal with those two drunks—the broken reco'd that they a'e. Always the same with those two. I'm really sta'tin' to lose my patience with 'em."

No matter how much her irritation rises, she sure loves hearing that strong Boston accent. So similar to Mainers. Brings back memories of better times back at their old business.

"Yeah, well, we might have to get used to these early arrivals," Lucy says. "We might also want to roll back on last call again, go to the old-school 1:00 AM deal. Hopefully that'll help get those two drunks outta here at a safer time."

"Damn! Tryin' to make my job even tougha, huh? Dave and Jerry will put up an even bigga protest with that."

"Yeah, well they can go fuck themselves. Those drunks have no idea how many times we've saved their asses from the hell spawns that roll through this place. Shit. We've saved this whole freakin' town from complete demonic destruction. Not one soul has been lost, thanks to us." She huffs, mumbles to herself, "If they only knew."

"Not yet anyway."

"I don't want to hear it again, Z. The tunnels are *not* getting sealed off. If *anyone* in my family survived the flares *and* the madness that followed, those tunnels are what saved them."

"Luce, think about it—With all those demons and creatures coming through the tunnels, if anyone in ya family *did* escape through the'a, what a'e the chances they survived run-ins with evil like *that*?"

A crooked, sly smirk appears on Lucy's face as she grabs her silver blade off the bar. "A question like that just shows you know *nothing* about my family." She steps out from behind the bar, re-clips the dagger to her belt, and motions with a head nod toward the backroom. "Let's go see how Zeppie's doing."

The *hush-hush* talk around old-Barning about the Vacca's and their witchy ways was never as quiet as the gabbers may have thought. The gossip plagued young Lucy. Bullies and their antics toughened her up, but at the same time, nastiness from the naysayers also softened her in a way. All her traumatic experiences created a humanitarian with a hidden dark side. She always looked out for the underdogs, the voice of reason in the face of potential violence, but she also honed some badass fighting skills—just in case.

Hence her ability with knives.

She had no way of knowing back then, but those bullies helped prepare her for the new world's tormentors—the raiders and the demons. Part of her feels thankful.

The ironic part—every time her family put on a solstice or equinox bonfire celebration, *every* bully in town had family members there. Maybe the bullying came from an attempt to keep themselves and their families out of the witchcraft gossip. That's always been Lucy's suspicion.

And you can bet your ass not one person ever questioned where the whiskey came from. No whiskey deliveries. No Vacca accounts with any local liquor stores. No travel for purchasing liquor elsewhere. Patrons just always expected whisky as a constant, always stocked. No one questioned. No one complained. Most everyone imbibed.

And those tunnels...Lucy was never allowed in the wine cellar alone, not even as a young adult home during vacations from Bennington College. Yes, she knew about the tunnels. A makeshift wooden wall was propped up in front of the one large opening back then. Her family told her the tunnels led to the old mines to the south and the west that were dangerous and off limits. Lucy always accepted that as truth. The one thing Lucy never questioned. She just never saw a reason for questioning it.

Until now.

Flickering flames of candlelight dance around the wine cellar as the thud of Lucy's boots clomp down the stairs. The closer she gets to the bottom, the faster her heartbeat revs up, wondering if anything else has snuck in yet. Her eyes dart all around the large space, searching for any unwanted visitors.

At the far end of the cellar, to her right, stands the tunnel opening. Though she looks there first, she knows evil doesn't always make a grand entrance. Evil likes to fly under the radar, hide where you'll least expect to find it.

She scans everywhere.

To her left sits the stock area. A wooden wine rack filled with bottled wine from the replenished Vacca's Vineyards stretches across one wall. All the dark bottles lying on their sides still wear the old Vacca's Vineyards' label, all worn and discolored from age. Though there's no need for labels on the liquor in a one-bar one-vineyard walled-in town of only three hundred people, Lucy insists on keeping them no matter how tattered they get.

Lucy may have a way about her that can frighten a grown man to tears and cause him to fall off bar stools and flee with his tail between his legs, but there's a hidden soft spot tucked away deep down inside her when it comes to those she cares about. Zeke and Zeppie have known this side of her since before the flares hit, since back in Maine when they worked for Lucy at her Weed Lounge and Caregiver Compound from the very first week she started the business.

Double Z. She's closer to those two than she'd ever been with any of her own blood.

When Zeppie, with his waist-length fat-dreaded hair and full beard, had first introduced himself at his job interview, Lucy instantly heard Ziggy Marley's "Power to Move Ya'" playing in her head. And Zeppie's chill 1970s hippie look—the icing on the Marley cake. Well, ever since that first impression he made on her, he's been her "Rasta Man." As for Zeke...just from the smell and appearance of a marijuana plant or bud that man can tell you the exact strain and what its medicinal makeup holds. He's a fucking weed genius—an inimitable member of their team—as well as a big cuddly teddy bear.

Protecting her Double Z is even more important to her than protecting the whole damned town.

Her keen eyes keep scanning the cellar for potential creepers.

Mounted to the floor, dead center between the wine rack and the opposite wall, sits that one mysterious oak whisky barrel. No matter how many bottles get filled from that barrel, somehow it's always full again when the need arises to fill more bottles. And no matter how tense she feels coming down here near The Devil's Hour, seeing that barrel always makes Lucy smile. Nonna's mysterious cookie jar also pops to mind.

Mama and Nonna—we have our ways.

The wall on the other side of the barrel has top-to-bottom built-in shelves lined with Mason jars, many filled with weed, some with tinctures, and others with various herb combinations. Affixed from one side of the room to the other, stretched out from the wine rack to the weed shelves, hang five strings. The crew hangs branches of marijuana plants here to dry before trimming and jarring the buds.

Face painted with surprise, Lucy notices all the bud-filled branches from earlier now lie stripped in a pile on the floor. And there's Zeppie, humming "Power to Move Ya" while he works. Down here pulling double-duty, stocking shelves and guarding tunnels–his workhorse way. His long, lean frame reaches to the highest shelf. No need for a step stool while he's around.

"Damn. You sure do know how to make the most of your time, now don't you?" Stepping over to him, she checks out all the freshly filled jars lining the shelves. "Sure hope nothing snuck in here while you were multitasking."

Zeppie turns around, looks down at her, gives her a slight elbow shove. "*Nothing* sneaks past me, Miss Hard-Ass." He smirks, shrugs, looks back at the shelves. "Gotta keep busy so I don't nod off. Can't have that happenin' when I know your internal demon radar has been going off like mad."

She rubs her temples with her fingertips. "Yeah, this ringing in my ears and throbbing in my head has picked up since that early arrival we vanquished. *Something* else is on its way, I just wish I knew what." She shakes off the discomfort, reaches out and grabs a Mason jar off one of the shelves. "So, I imagine you've already taken care of the wine section if you're jarring up the buds now?"

"Got that done earlier tonight, just forgot to mention it."

She reaches up and pats him on the back. "Man, I can always count on you to help keep this ship afloat."

Zeppie's contagious smile spreads wide amidst his black forest of a beard. "I'm not the only one bustin' my ass around here, Lucifer." He winks.

When the demons began appearing, he started calling her Queen of the Underworld. Add in the discovery of the whisky barrel somehow refilling itself, then Lucy's nickname changed to Lucifer.

Makes sense to her. She was the one in her family who didn't follow the rules, the one misunderstood and cast out—sort of.

As tense as things get around here at this time of night, it doesn't stop that warm feeling that washes over her every time she hears Zeppie call her by her nickname.

She met a couple of good eggs back on her own in Maine.

Without her Double Z, Lucy has no idea how she would've ever got Vacca's Vineyards back up and producing. Then planting and working the marijuana crops—she wouldn't've trusted *anyone* else in town to follow through with that business venture. And her family never would've approved. But Double Z knew. They knew how desperately the people of Barning needed the medicinal treatment her miracle plants could provide, even if the people didn't know it yet themselves. It worked out for everyone that she and her guys had thought to bring a seed-filled jar from their underground harvest center back in Maine. That little construction idea saved their asses when the flares hit, the planes dropped, and the fires spread. Thankfully, the valley of Barning had been spared, and her old homestead still stood, waiting, almost calling for her to come home.

Underground survival–she holds hope her family did the same, escaping the raiders during the early aftermath.

Specializing in wine and weed and whisky, the Silver Blade Saloon had almost been named WWW.Wonderland. But when people caught wind of that idea it made them miss having computers and the internet—not to mention basic electricity. Then the town heard of Lucy's way with throwing knives, and people started calling her The Silver Blade Slinger. The rest is history.

From behind Lucy, Zeke's footfalls thud down the stairs. Just as he reaches the bottom step, Lucy turns and tosses him the Mason jar filled with an ounce of fresh weed.

"Don't forget your pay from last harvest." She smiles. "You might wanna bring that upstairs for safekeeping before more creepers come skulking through." She nods toward the far end of the cellar where the tunnel entrance hangs open like the mouth of a hungry beast ready to devour.

"Dude, mind bringin' mine upstairs too?" Towering over Lucy as though she's a child, Zeppie leans over, holds out another weed-filled jar. "Just finished jarring up the final buds. Less work tomorrow." He cocks one eyebrow, smirks. "You're welcome, Stoney."

"Haw, haw...Thanks, man. I don't ca'e what anyone says—you the best!" Zeke reciprocates the smirk, pops out his hand for a fist-bump, then grabs the other Mason jar.

Zeppie's long dreads sway like a beaded curtain as he motions with his head toward the dark gaping hole on the other end of the cellar. "No prob, but hurry back. Don't go gettin' distracted up there. We need to be ready, stick together."

"You got it." Zeke hightails it up the stairs, skipping steps like a jumping jackrabbit. Everyone around here knows weed doesn't slow this guy down. It's just what he needs to mellow his anxiety enough to stay in this fucked-up game of survival.

Scouting around the cellar, looking behind boxes and under extra chairs and tables, Lucy wonders how much longer they can keep the creatures from getting to the folks in town. Those sneaky tricksters. When Zeppie was lugging stock up from downstairs earlier tonight, he spotted a creeper hiding behind the open cellar door. No idea *what* it was. Without Zeppie's calm demeanor, the salt circle trap never would've gotten set up without *it* noticing. But that's Zeppie—the most chill of the bunch, even without weed. Add in a silver blade slice and dice, and that creeper's sorry-ass story ended before it could make it out the back door.

What if Zeppie hadn't spotted it hiding? What if it had made it outside? The townsfolk out there sleeping nice and cozy, unsuspecting, like a gourmet buffet spread out for these soulless fuckers that sneak out from the dark recesses of the underground.

Yeah, Lucy supposes closing the bar earlier might help, but rolling back on last call again is sure to push people to ask questions, especially Dave and Jerry.

The vineyards need earlier tending in the mornings, yeah. She hears how phony her anticipated excuse sounds in her head. Will anyone believe her?

"Don't you think it's time to seal up those tunnels...seal up those tunnels...seal up those tunnels?"

Every time she seriously considers closing off that tunnel entrance, an unbearable ache squeezes her chest.

A loud *bang-crash* sounds from upstairs.

Zeke?!

Thuds.

Scuffling.

Knife in hand before she has time to blink, Lucy hightails it up the stairs, tells Zeppie, "Stay back and watch the tunnels. Whatever's up there could just be a distraction."

Zeppie's words sound out from behind her. "Yeah, but what if..."

"I'll yell if we need you." A quick glance over her shoulder. Zeppie pulls his foot back off the bottom step.

The first thing she sees when she steps out of that stairwell–the barn-style doors in the backroom flung open to the night. A strong wind howls, whips one door against the building. *Bang-Crash.* The same sound that signaled trouble.

A narrow beam of moonlight creeps across the floor. Two mangled mounds lie in the silvery glow, pools of blood, tubes of intestines snaking around the bodies like a chaotic infinity knot.

She rushes over. Her blade arrives first, swinging around, pointing this way and that, making sure whatever caused this isn't ready to pounce and rearrange her like the mounds on the floor. Whoever or whatever they are—or were—she hasn't had a chance to make that determination.

Two gunshot blasts tear through the air.

The deafening sound rips at her eardrums. Sounds close. From outside.

Where the fuck is Zeke?

With hopes it was his gun she'd just heard, a fear of human raiders still slowly creeps over her. Memories from their treacherous journey from Maine to Barning flash across her mind. A quick glance at the mounds beside her feet, then immediately back outside, ready and waiting for whatever comes next.

No doubt the town's waking up right about now. No one knows they had old-world guns and ammo hidden on them when they traveled from Maine. These Three Amigos have tried their best to keep shooting at a minimum—keep the locals from questioning. But sometimes...well, sometimes they've just got to do what they've got to do to keep people safe.

Suddenly, a burly silhouette emerges outside the double doors, progressing forward with the moonlight at its back. It appears as nothing but a tall, bulky shadow lumbering toward her.

She squints, shifts her position, draws her blade back, aims.

The shadow shape has arms. It holds them out to its sides, raises them up as though under arrest.

That's no demon.

That's Zeke.

Head hung low, he shambles toward her, says nothing. He arrives beside her and the bloody mounds upon the floor.

"Are you alright? Where's the demon? Did you get it? Did it get outside? Was it just one, or are there more?"

He only nods.

She dashes behind him, pulls the double doors shut, locks them, rushes back to his side.

"What does that mean, Zeke?" Grasping his arm, she pulls him close, brushes his shaggy dreads out of his face. There's a coating of charcoal gray dust caked into the sweat all over his face, neck, and arms.

She wipes away some dust from around his eyes, brushes her hand off on her jeans. Seeing the dust confirms her demon idea. Zeke must've vaporized it. Her shoulders relax a bit.

Until he finally speaks.

He crouches down near the mounds beside their feet. "Demon's done. But so a'e Dave and Jerry." Shaking his head, he squeezes his eyes shut, pinches his lips with a dusty hand.

A sudden squeezing sensation hits Lucy's entire body. A python-style hug.

"No. That can't be. How? They went home a while..." Voice catching in her throat, she focuses her eyes more intensely on the mounds, willing those bloody bodies into wild animals rather than two Barning townies she sees and talks to every day. Men with families, kids, friends.

There must've been two demons earlier. One that did get outside somehow.

Boot knife in hand, Zeke reaches toward one of the mounds, eases the blade under what looks like—

"Incoming!" Zeppie's voice bellows up the cellar stairs. "All hands on deck!"

Lucy grabs Zeke's shoulder. "Leave 'em. Let's go!"

As quick as a blink, he follows Lucy's lead.

They both thunder down the cellar stairs.

As soon as they make it halfway down, Lucy notices Zeppie, silver-bullet-loaded double barrel sawed-off shotgun in hand, standing beside the mouth of the tunnel. She and Zeke rush over to assist.

Twenty or so feet inside the tunnel something lurks in the shadows. Writhing and growling sounds emanate from its direction. Lucy progresses closer, Zeke at her heels. Then she holds out her silver blade and stands in the center of the gaping hole. Zeke, revolver replacing the blade in hand, steps off to the opposite side of the entrance from Zeppie.

Zeppie reaches behind him for a lit lantern, hands it to Lucy.

Lantern in one hand, knife in the other, Lucy steps into the tunnel. A wave of flickering light shines almost far enough to see what, or who, remains hidden. Some kind of mound at the corner of the offshoot tunnel strategically blocks Lucy's view.

Knife held out in front, Lucy takes a wide-legged fighter's stance. She bellows, "We know you're there! It's time to show yourself!" She moves the lantern around, tries casting light on what lies ahead.

Movement. Very slight movement from the shadow. More growling, though quieter, a low rumble. Sounds almost like a wounded animal.

Something about this seems familiar.

Lucy steps deeper inside, moves the lantern around more, leans forward for a better look.

A glimpse of black hair. Long. Wavy. Wild and moving all around, as though from gusting winds. But no wind blows underground. Lucy imagines tentacles or snakes.

"What are you doing, Luce? Remember, let it come to us." Zeppie steps up behind her, reaches out, touches her shoulder. He whispers, "Let it come to us."

She brushes his hand away, takes another step forward.

The rumbling growl stops. A quiet weeping replaces it, followed by a gasp as what appears to be a woman with long hair as black as a starless new-moon night steps out of the shadows.

The voice that comes from it is low, gravelly, and...

It sounds human.

"Lucy? Is that you? My Lucy-loo?"

Lucy's throat tightens, chest aches, eyes sting. Not even Double Z knows her childhood nickname.

"Mom?" Lucy's knife wielding hand lowers to her side. Another step forward. Lantern held high to get a better look. "Is that you, Mom?"

The woman takes painfully slow steps further out of the shadows into the lantern light.

She appears just as Lucy remembers her. Short and thin with long black hair. She's even wearing the same sunflower sundress Lucy had bought her for the last birthday they'd ever celebrated together. The last visit home Lucy had taken to celebrate her mom's fifty-fifth birthday, three months before the flares first hit.

The woman from the shadows nods slowly, smiles. She holds out her arms, starts walking closer.

Lucy's knife drops from her hand, thuds against the dirt-covered ground.

Though she hesitates for a moment, Lucy follows the woman's lead, as though in a trance. Without looking away, she blindly sets the lantern on a rocky outcropping of the tunnel wall. It wobbles, teetering on the edge. Her arms raise out in front of her, ready for a hug, as she moves slowly toward the woman.

From behind, Zeke and Zeppie move to the center of the tunnel's entrance. They both speak at once.

Zeke: "No, Luce. Don't listen. Stay back."

Zeppie: "Lucy, your mother should be seventy-five years old. That's not her!"

"Mom, I kept the tunnels open for you. I've missed you so..."

"Stop, Lucy." Shotgun still aimed at the in-coming woman, Zeppie rushes up behind Lucy. Without taking his eyes off what lies ahead, he leans down near her ear. "Look at her feet, Lucifer. That's *not* your mother."

With a swing of her elbow, Lucy pushes him away, ignores his words, progresses forward.

He falters, loses aim. With a quick readjustment he's back at Lucy's heels, gun aimed ahead of them. "You know you can trust me, Lucifer. I'm your Rasta Man. Just *look* at her *feet*."

My Rasta...

Lucy hesitates, shakes her head, looks down toward the ground.

Her mother has no feet.

She has hooves.

Lucy rubs her eyes. Wonders if her tears have distorted her vision. When she raises them back up to look the woman in the face...

Those eyes.

More shock takes hold. Lucy expects to see piercing blue staring back at her. But instead, she sees nothing but pure black. Black holes ready to devour all.

Before anyone has time to react, the still-smiling woman claps. Snuffs out the light. Growls and pounces. Two deafening shotgun blasts rend through the air.

Soft, flickering light from the relit lantern hanging from Zeke's shaky hand illuminates—

Zeppie.

Lying on the ground, not moving.

Some sort of black oily substance drenches him, dripping from his dreads and shimmering on the toes of his beat-up combat boots. Chunks and pebbles from the bullet-punctured rock ceiling speckle his body like stars in an obsidian sky.

Down on one knee, Lucy, also splattered with black goo, crouches beside him. Clenched in the hand of her frozen-in-mid-strike right arm—her backup boot knife. The one blessed by Father Jose and dipped in a tincture of basil, rue, and rosemary. A concoction known for centuries to aid against spiritual evils. (Holy water alone doesn't always work. A mixture of faiths holds more power.) Still on guard, she looks all around, making sure the shapeshifter is truly gone.

Zeke, lantern in one hand and revolver in the other, rushes up, holds the light over Zeppie's body.

Beside Zeppie's head rests a large rock. Across his forehead is a laceration. Across his stomach rests the empty double barrel shotgun, his fingers still clenched around the triggers.

Lucy shakes him. "Zep? Hey, man, can you hear me? Zeppie?"

Nothing. No response.

Pounding in her head, she hears the maddening sound of her own revved-up heartbeat.

She leans down close, puts her right ear to his chest. Gazing toward his head wound as she listens for a heartbeat, she cups the side of his face in her hand. Her heart is beating so hard, so loud, she can't tell if *his* heart still beats. She feels around for a pulse. There's just so much black goo. And it's thick.

"I don't unda'stand—where'd the shapeshifter go?" Though he stands close with the lantern, Zeke keeps nervously looking all around, as though ready for an ambush. "And what the hell is all ova' you two?"

Lucy holds up her boot knife. "I liquified that conniving bitch." She throws a glance at the black goo all over Zeppie and spattered on her. She wipes the boot knife on a clean spot on the side of her bustier before she re-sheathes it. "I *guess* this is all that's left of it. Huh..." She holds out her arm, quickly inspects the sticky black stuff everywhere. "A lot different than dust remains, that's for sure."

Zeke, expression difficult to read, nods, looks back down at his buddy splayed out on the ground with a gash on his head. "Is he bleeding?"

"He's *gotta* be...There's just so much of this black shit everywhere I can't tell how *much* he's bleeding." She cups the side of his face again, leans in closer, starts gently wiping the demon remains from around his wound. That's when she feels it.

This close to his face, Lucy feels his breath.

"He's breathing. He's fucking breathing, dude!" She starts shaking him again. "Zeppie, wake up. We're here. Please...wake up." Cleaning around his wound again, she feels a different consistency to the demon remains closest to the injury.

Blood.

Lots of it. Mixed with the black sticky liquid.

"Towels." She hesitates a moment, not sure what to do first. "Grab me some towels. I need to slow the bleeding."

No hesitation, Zeke bolts back into the cellar, leaving the lantern behind for his friends.

His family.

Minutes later, wound cleaner and bleeding slowing down, they've moved Zeppie out of the tunnel and into the wine cellar, head cushioned by Lucy's lap. She runs her fingers, now soaked with lavender oil to help revive him, gently along his hairline, brushing stray dreads off his face.

As he's leaning over his unconscious brother, wondering when—or if—he'll ever wake up, Zeke, joint puckered between his lips, inhales a little sanity to calm his nerves.

Slowly, chest aching and head numb, Lucy starts rocking side-to-side as she quietly sings "You are my sunshine" over and over again, as though she's soothing a crying baby. Just like her mother used to do for little Lucy-loo.

She doesn't know what else to do. He has to wake up.

Her voice hitches, crackles.

She looks up at Zeke, sees his watery eyes, knee bouncing, nervous smoke rings puffing out, wavering in the air above his head. Back down to Zeppie, eyes closed, head resting in her lap, gash across his forehead, bloody towels beside him.

Her chest aches to think of losing her Double Z. Even one of them. The three of them together, The Three Amigos—they're inseparable, a powerhouse, a team...a family. They've helped one another through the worst possible circumstances this world could've thrown at them, and still they stand strong by each other's sides. Zeke may not realize it, but it's taking all her strength to keep from crumbling. She's not ready to lose another loved one. She thought she just found her mom, only to realize her stubborn insistence on keeping those tunnels open might be what takes a member of her new family—her chosen family.

A tear falls, splashes on Zeppie's forehead. Still rocking him, Lucy leans down close to his ear. "*Please* wake up. You can't leave us...me. You're my Rasta Man." The wind of her whisper blows a strand of her hair across his wounded face. Squeezing her eyes shut, trying to seal up the damn, she repeats, "You'll always be my Rasta, no matter what."

A big puff of skunky smoke fills her nostrils. Zeke is all of a sudden crouched down beside them.

"His hand just moved." He reaches out, grasps Zeppie's arm.

A slight breeze circles around them, tussles their hair. Puzzled, they look at each other, cautious curiosity in their eyes.

Is there another uninvited visitor coming?

At the exact same moment, they both glance across the room at the tunnel. Zeke fumbles around behind him for his revolver. Hand on the hilt of her blade, Lucy's ready for whatever might dare venture its way into the cellar.

"Man, that was close."

They both freeze. Look back to one another. Look down toward Lucy's lap.

Half open, Zeppie's eyes roll from Zeke to Lucy.

He sniffs. "Is that lavender? Am I alive?"

His friends nod.

Zeppie's eyes open wider. "Please tell me you ganked that shifter."

Silent, lips pinched tight, clamping down the emotions, Lucy smiles, nods, runs her fingers down his hair.

"Thank..."

A sudden hug interrupts Zeppie's words.

The next day, before any of the three head out to the vineyards or the marijuana crop, Lucy asks Double Z to meet her in the wine cellar. For the first time ever, Zeke arrives first.

"Zeppie's alright, I hope."

He nods. "Changing the bandage on his fo'ehead."

"Aha." She glances away toward the tunnel side of the cellar. "Stitches are holdin' up okay?"

"You know, Luce, if you weren't so quick on the draw, Zeppie would've been a goner last night."

Her boots clomp across the cement floor. "And Dave and Jerry?" Pausing, she glances over her shoulder toward him.

With a somber expression, Zeke leans against the whisky barrel. "Moved to the woods but not too far in. Looks like an animal attack."

She nods. "Thank you." Turning back around, she walks further across the cellar. "That's good. Easy to find. Proper burials should help give closure to loved ones, respect to the fallen."

She stops next to a stack of crates, bends down and rifles around behind it. Zeke moves closer, stands so near behind her she almost bumps into him when she straightens back upright.

He opens his mouth, just about to say something, when Lucy turns and faces him.

"Less talk, more work." She shoves a toolbox into his stomach.

Though confused, he grabs the box.

Footfalls thud down the cellar stairs, accompanied by cheerful singing—Ziggy Marley's "It's Just a Beautiful Day."

"Sun's up over the trees. A beautiful day to work the crops. Why are we wasting our time underground?" Zeppie steps off the staircase with a beaming smile bright enough to light the whole damn town of Barning on the darkest of nights.

Lucy reaches behind the stack of crates and hauls out a couple of long wooden planks. "Today's work is down here."

She drops the boards beside her Double Z. Now smiles beam on each of their faces.

Zeke pulls out a joint from over his ear, lights it, inhales, passes it on. When the shared toke ends, the Three Amigos get right to work.

The patrons of The Silver Blade Saloon may get pissed when they find out about the last-minute closure for the day, but that's better than the alternative.

Before the doors open back up for business later that night, a brand-new wall stands tall, closing up the tunnel opening. Exhausted but eager for a less stressful kind of business, Lucy and Zeke and Zeppie head up the cellar stairs.

The door at the top of the stairs clicks shut behind them. Relieved, the Three Amigos strut confidently out into the barroom, light the lanterns, unlock the front door and usher in the first customers of the night who have gathered on the porch, waiting.

Down in the dark depths of the wine cellar, there comes a scratching and pounding at the new tunnel wall. Grunts and wailing cries accompany the sounds.

"Hello! Are you there? Lucy-loo? Help us!"

No one is there to hear the cacophony.

Sepia

Chloe Viner

Life is sepia-colored
grays browns and dark reds
sap trickling down bark
anxieties exude from skin
jagged slices hewn from my arms
dark brown soaked rivets
bleakness bleeds from my skin
food is flavorless
thoughts have dulled points
not the road less traveled by
I have been here many times before
most red berries are safe to eat
but nothing bright speckles the landscape
abandoned farmhouses and broken gates
I sit between two oaks and know
the sun will set
and nothing new
will rise tomorrow

Broken Hart

Franklin Ard

The day of my deliverance, I'm wearing my lucky grave boots. It's just Jamie and me cruising the outskirts of Barning in an our solar-powered Plymouth De Luxe. Jamie, being the gearhead that he is, rigged up the solar panels to catch all the sun's rays—the same rays that burned up so much of the world—and recharge the car battery. But salvaging the panels and putting them to good use? That was my idea.

That's why Jamie and me make such a great pair. We complement each other. You might say that we were made for one another. That is, if you believe in such things. I don't believe in much, but I do believe in destiny. Sometimes, destiny leads us to someone cracked-up who needs mending. Other times, we're the ones destined to be broken. With Jamie, it's a bit of both.

The wind pinwheels my hair and there's glass at my feet because Jamie busted the passenger window when we took the jalopy from the junkyard. He steps on the gas, not watching the road. His eyes are set in shadows. Since getting shot during a bank robbery two days ago, he's been awful brazen. The bullet hole in his shoulder missed his heart by a good four inches, and now he acts like he's invincible.

He's started talking about how he thinks he can escape his own demise. It ain't just that he skirted death. It's more than that. You see, Jamie's been convinced for years that he'd die of a broken heart. It's all because of an epiphany he had as a kid. Jamie and me, our parents were originally from the South before The Burn, so we have this kind of bond, almost like we're brothers in a way. Although we were both born in Barning, we still have Southern accents because of our parents, though Jamie's is thicker because his family comes from Mississippi.

Jamie shouts to me over the wind: "You'll never be free until you learn how you're supposed to go, Kid. Once you know, you can tell the grim reaper to fuck off."

He's all the time calling me Kid, even though that ain't my real name. He's done it for months, but I don't mind. It's just what I go by now.

The faster the Plymouth careens, the more trouble Jamie has controlling it. The spare tire rattles in the trunk, sounding like a broken refrigerator. I spot a horse-drawn wagon coming our way in the opposite lane. It isn't one of those fancy stagecoaches that a few people have. It's just cobbled together from hunks of old wood, stacked fifteen feet high with heavy bags of flour and other supplies. The horses struggle to pull the wagon, looking underfed. However, the man steering the wagon doesn't appear to have ever missed a meal.

Jamie says, "You'd really like to know right now, wouldn't you? You want to know how you're gonna go. Ain't that right?"

"I don't know," I say.

"But you want to," Jamie says.

"I guess I am curious about it," I say.

Jamie twists the steering wheel, and we swerve toward the wagon.

"What are you doing?" I scream, gripping my seat.

"It's about time you had your own epiphany. You can't stick with me unless you've played the game of death and won. I need a partner who ain't afraid."

The wagon tries to veer, but Jamie keeps us head-on. We go so fast that the broken pavement rocks kick up around the Plymouth's tires. The dust makes it so I can't see the man's face, but I imagine that he's crying, his cheeks fat and red and wet because he knows we're going to plow right into him.

But it's not him who's crying. It's me, tasting the salt of my own tears.

"Tell me you want to know," Jamie says.

I don't answer at first. The horses neigh and clamor forward, putting themselves further in danger. The wagon driver yells something that's all garbled and sounds like Morse code.

I speak up, timid: "I want to know."

"Goddamn it!" Jamie shouts over the wind. "Tell me like you mean it."

I take a deep dusty breath and bellow: "I want to know!"

"What do you want to know?" Jamie asks, his scraggly dirty blond hair flailing in the wind.

The wagon turns, just about toppling over sideways, and our Plymouth barrels onward. I try to push an imaginary brake in the floorboard.

I tremble, feeling nauseous. "I want to know how I'll die."

"Time's running out," Jamie says.

Imagining the crunch of metal, the crack of wood, and then the bloody flesh of those horses, I get desperate. I long for the same kind of clarity Jamie had all those years ago. I really do want to know. I want to see the end flash before my eyes just the way it did for him.

"Say something, Kid," Jamie yells. "Do you see it? The epiphany?"

Our bumper almost touching the wagon, I call out my answer: "I have it! I know, Jamie!"

He spins the wheel, and we slam into the ditch. My forehead hits the dashboard and blood runs down my nose. The horses and the man make equally manic sounds as the wagon pulls away. The smoke from the communal fires of Barning billows in our rearview mirror. People keep the fires burning day and night, so people without fireplaces in their homes, or without homes at all, have a place to cook and keep warm.

"So, how're you gonna go?" Jamie asks, resting his forehead against the steering wheel.

In the moment of fear, I'd lied. I didn't have an epiphany. Really, the only thing I know about how I'll leave this world is that I'll go out by Jamie's side. With nothing to say, I play pretend. I look at him with spaced-out eyes, as though I'd just learned some great cosmic secret about the universe, hoping to convince him that I believe in near-death epiphanies as strongly as he does.

"I'm going to die of a broken heart too," I say, through gritted teeth.

Jamie wipes his mouth, looks at the crimson smear on the back of his hand, and laughs. "I guess this makes us blood brothers."

Yesterday, I saw the cross. Jamie and me were washing up in Icebox Creek, one of several frigid tributaries of the Green River. The waters foamed with soapsuds, and I kept one eye on the woods because there was no telling when Sheriff Reginald's boys would try to spring a trap on us. What a way to go that would be—naked in a shallow creek on the edge of Goose Mountain.

I finished scrubbing my face. "We need to clean that wound of yours."

Jamie shook his head. "Ain't no *we* about it."

"You'll need help stitching up," I said, sloshing closer.

I dragged my fingertips along his muscular shoulder, and he splashed backward, eyes big and startled like he was looking at a dead man. "I told you not to touch me again," he snarled.

I'd saved his life during the bank robbery, and I'd manhandled him to do it. He still hadn't forgiven me. Jamie hated owing another person anything.

He punched me with his good arm, and I went down in a splash. He was on top of me in seconds. The water blocked the force of his fist, but I winced and yelled out anyway. As long as Jamie thought he was hurting me, he wouldn't stop.

I blocked his punches until he tired out and we both sat in the shallow water, watching the minnows. Then I glanced up and saw something between the trees.

"Look over there," I said, pointing. "In the woods."

Jamie froze. "Cops?"

"River grave," I said.

Jamie's been chasing Confederate gold for years. He has this idea that a fortune was secretly smuggled north when the Rebels fled Richmond during the latter days of the Civil War, and that some of the gold is hidden somewhere in our neck of the woods here in Vermont.

Spotting the cross among the pines, he slapped my chest. "You're all right, Kid."

Gold was the reason Jamie had gotten shot in the first place. Ronnie Younger, a local boy who fancied himself an old-time outlaw, told us the Barning Bank & Trust had pure Confederate yellow in its vault. Ronnie heard this from his cousin who had some inside info. The three of us formed a posse, which we called the James-Younger Gang, and robbed that bank. We left with enough gold bullion to keep us afloat for a few months. Not the mythical Confederate gold, but still nothing to sneeze at.

But Jamie, he also left with a broken heart.

We dressed in the sand. My shoes were wet, so I went barefoot up the steep hill. The grave was old, unearthed by rainstorms over the years, the cross leaning. A sun-browned skeleton lay partway covered in dead leaves.

"Jamie, am I really seeing what I think I'm seeing?" I said, my breath catching with excitement.

Jamie's mouth hung open for a second. "Yeah, you are, Kid."

Tatters of a Confederate flag clung to the skeleton's ribcage. The glossed riding boots sitting beside its feet hadn't decayed, I guess because the hill had protected the gravesite from water damage. We stood there in reverence for a few moments as the sun beat down on us. Though chill air swept through the trees, the sun's intensity seemed to grow. Townsfolk had been murmuring lately about more solar flares hitting us, but no one knew anything for sure.

"This could be our big jackpot," Jamie said, stepping into the grave.

"Be careful," I said, squishing dirt between my toes.

Jamie grinned like a gambler as he pulled a molding journal from inside a little metal box in the skeleton's arms. I watched over Jamie's shoulder as he opened the leather cover. Names webbed across the browned paper in tiny script, forming a sideways tree, their dates of death recorded to the day. I read the tree of names aloud. *Jefferson Davis* was written in cursive on the trunk, and the note-taker had recorded that the President died in 1889 of fever.

Jamie leafed through the pages. The name *Bottlecap Murphy* was recorded in nervous penmanship at the bottom of the last page. No year of death.

"What do you make of it?" Jamie asked.

"It's some kind of genealogy chart," I replied.

"I recognize some of these names from my readings," Jamie said, his face flushing. "It's the family line of Jefferson Davis." Jamie knows a lot about history for a man who never stepped foot in a schoolhouse.

"Who was this bag of bones?" I asked. "A Rebel soldier who traveled north?"

"Not possible," Jamie said. "This man lived until at least The Collapse. See, he recorded this man, Bottlecap Murphy's, date of birth and then some details about his upbringing."

"That makes sense," I said.

Jamie scratched his chin. "Bones could have been a Rebel soldier's descendent, though. Maybe one of those weirdos who still wanted the

Confederates to regroup and rise again. There are people like that, even now that the world has gone to hell."

"But why was he tracking Jefferson Davis' family?"

"Five of the President's children died young," Jamie said. "Bones might've been trying to protect what was left of the line."

We stood there in silence for a moment, looking at the decrepit skeleton.

"Or maybe Bones here was searching for something," Jamie said, a faraway look in his eye. "Maybe he was on the trail of the Confederate gold that Jefferson Davis directed his men to sneak north at the end of the War." Jamie picked up the dead man's riding boots and handed them to me. "Put these on while I get my pack. Can't beat a good pair of boots, and yours are falling apart."

I did as Jamie directed while he hiked back to the shore. He returned carrying his leather satchel. I stood over him as he kneeled, fished around in his pack, and retrieved six of the seven gold ingots we'd stolen from the bank. He tucked them among the remains.

"Safe keeping, in case things get wild on the trail," he said. "No one but us will know where these are buried, and we'll come back for them after things settle down."

"Where're we going?" I asked, flexing my ankles in the boots. They were a perfect fit.

"We need to find Bottlecap Murphy," Jamie said. "He's the end of the line."

I remembered that no date of death had been recorded for Bottlecap Murphy. Bottlecap must've still been alive when Bones finally kicked the bucket himself. "We find Bottlecap, we find the gold," I said.

"That's right," Jamie said. He started down the hill, holding the journal under his arm like a schoolboy. "I think it's time we paid Violet the banker a visit."

We finally got around to paying Violet the banker a visit after Jamie tried to kill me in the car. Violet isn't actually a banker. Jamie just calls her that. She works at the Barning Bank & Trust as a clerk, but she does basically keep the whole place running.

Jamie cuts the headlights as we roll up to her rickety house. He does that so we can stake things out without being noticed, but also because the beams drain the battery fast. Even with a pissed-off sun during the day, the solar panels on the roof can only collect so much light and store so much energy for nighttime.

Jamie scratches. That's his nervous tic before something big is about to go down, and I know what he has in mind. As much as I can predict Jamie, the thing I can't do is stop his momentum. The Plymouth lurches to a stop, and my skin crawls.

A kerosene lamp inside Violet's house casts carnival colors behind the window screen. A shadow shaped like a gargoyle moves across the wall, limbs swinging.

"What's going on in there?" I ask.

Jamie kills the engine. "Looks like her boyfriend's in a fighting mood."

Violet screams.

"You think he's a boozer?"

Jamie grits his teeth. "If he is, that ain't no excuse."

Jamie's daddy beat a hard spot into Jamie's heart, and that's when Jamie had his epiphany about his future death. Nowadays, getting back at abusers is how he softens up that hard spot inside of him. But that's not the only reason we're visiting Violet.

"Robbing a town bank is one thing," I whisper, "but I'm not sure what you're planning is a good idea."

Jamie opens the car door and hops out. "Well, it's a good thing nobody asked you." He picks up a horseshoe-sized rock, runs forward, and ducks under the windowsill.

I get out and make my way across the dark grass and crouch beside him. "How well do we really know this girl? I mean, especially after what she did back at the bank robbery."

"Doesn't matter about that. I have a good feeling about her. Just back me up, Kid," he says, running his hand over his scraggly hair. He tosses the rock through the screen and climbs inside.

Seeing Jamie make his entrance, Violet's boyfriend roars. The guy is ripped like a grizzly bear. I shake my head, knowing this isn't going to end well, and flip over the sill and land on my back. Violet crawls toward me. She's barefoot in a calico dress. Her hair looks blue in the lamplight, and her right eye is blacked. Her cheek is so swollen I can't make out the freckles.

Her boyfriend grabs Jamie by the shirt and slams him against the wall. "Who do you think you are?" the guy yells, pinning his forearm against Jamie's neck. "You want my girl. Is that it?"

"Do something," Violet says to me.

I stand up and ball my fist.

"You don't wanna do that, my man." The boyfriend's sandy blonde hair is greased with sweat.

Jamie knees him in the groin, then rams the guy's forehead against an exposed wall stud. The boyfriend rocks back, dizzy on his heels, and thuds on the wood floor.

Jamie picks up the rock and glares at the boyfriend's face.

"He's already out cold," I say.

Violet whispers in my ear. "Let your friend take care of my little problem."

Jamie drops the rock, steps away from the boyfriend, and turns to Violet. "Now that we've saved your ass, you'd better tell us what we want to know."

She snarls her lip at me then turns back to Jamie. "You didn't finish the job."

"You can do that yourself if you want," Jamie says. "I've got other concerns."

Violet twirls her dark hair. "Like what?"

Jamie takes a step forward. "More like *who*."

"Bottlecap Murphy," I say.

"What about him?" Violet asks.

"He come to your bank?" Jamie asks.

She nods. "Sure does."

"Tell us where to find him," I say.

Violet steps close to Jamie, her nose almost touching his. "No."

Jamie's leg twitches. "What did you say?"

"I won't tell you," Violet says, jabbing a finger at his chest. "But I'll take you there."

The first time I called Sheriff Reginald was right after washing in the creek. Jamie and me went to Bobby's Place to get some of Dot's slap-your-mouth Johnnycakes, which we could now afford thanks to the remaining gold ingot that we'd held onto. Jamie had used a lug wrench from the Plymouth's trunk to break the ingot into several pieces that we could use to pay for things around Barning.

Bobby's Place had been around for a while, the only drinking establishment to rival the Silver Blade Saloon, but it was a real dump. I always thought Bobby should advertise it as grungy pub or something like that. The Johnnycakes were literally the best thing I'd venture to put in my stomach at Bobby's, aside from the homebrew beer, and that was thanks to Dot's excellent skills in the kitchen. Bobby had done well in hiring her to cook.

Jamie always wanted to be part of the rougher scene in town. If it wasn't for his obsession with Confederate gold, I think he would have spent all his time at the saloon or the brothel down the street. The brothel was called Smokey Joe's Basement, and you had to go down a steep flight of stairs to find the action. The guy who owned the joint was named Casey, and he always wore a kimono and big, gaudy earrings. His hair was so blond that it made your eyes hurt looking at his locks. He had an infectious smile that would light up the entire room if someone told a joke. Upon figuring out that the guy loved puns, Jamie spent hours at the library, reading up on humor to get on Casey's good side. That's how he got Casey to let us into the brothel whenever we wanted, even though we were technically underage.

Jamie wanted to hit the saloon mostly to lose money at poker, but I hated going in there. Rumor had it the place was cursed. The talk of town was that the curse was due to some strange creatures that lived in the old mining tunnels that ran underneath the building and out the other side of Barning. The creatures were possibly people who'd been mutated by some gnarly solar radiation during the worst days of The Burn, though some of the locals called the creatures demons. Word had it that these creatures had supernatural powers. But I didn't really believe that. Bobby, on the other hand, swore on his mother's grave that the demons were real.

While Dot made our Johnnycakes, Bobby regaled Jamie with a story about the last time he'd gotten a wild hair and ventured to the tunnels. "The fuckin' things'll eat your face off. I'm telling you, man," he said, gesturing with his broad hands.

Meanwhile, I went to the bathroom. Bobby's Place is one of the only spots in town where you can find toilet paper anymore. Dot makes the paper from dried leaves, and I planned to take full advantage of it.

The other thing Bobby's is known for is being one of the only buildings in town with a functioning telephone. Select places in Barning had them, and calls could only be made to other establishments within Barning. Basically, it saved people a walk across town on days the sun was particularly destructive. You could trace which buildings had a phone by following the drooping lines strung between the roofs. Though Bobby talked too much, he allowed the public to use his phone anytime they wanted, which made him okay in my book.

On my way to the bathroom, my mind played back the bank robbery, how during the heist Jamie had pointed a revolver at Violet's head. I remembered her crying and giggling at the same time. I wasn't really sure what Jamie was capable of, and my nerves did get to me sometimes.

In a moment of weakness, feeling that I may be in over my head, I sneaked over and spun the dial on the phone. Since there were only a handful of places with phones, the number to the sheriff's office was just the digit four.

"Sheriff speaking." He sounded timid when saying *sheriff*, like the word didn't feel right coming out of his mouth. Sheriff Reginald had only taken over the job a month before, after Sheriff Bethany had retired due to some kind of scandal.

The old phone crackled. "This is Billy the Kid."

"No shit," Sheriff said. "And I'm Mickey fucking Mouse."

"Who the hell is that?" I asked.

"Forget I mentioned it," Sheriff said.

I paused, then added a bit of gruffness to my voice to sound older and tougher. "I'm one of the boys who robbed the Barning Bank & Trust."

The sheriff's voice perked up. "Calling to turn yourself in, son?"

"Just throwing you a bone for the chase. I'm calling you from the diner. Ask Bobby where he got the hunk of gold ingot." With that, I hung up. I couldn't bear the idea of Jamie doing anything to hurt anyone else, whether they deserved it or not. If he was going to hurt someone, I wanted it to be me.

Jamie's driving, and Violet's his passenger. I'm the strongman, holding onto Violet's shoulder and keeping an eye on her from the backseat. Full-throttling down the potholed road, Jamie isn't watching where he's going. I catch him looking up Violet's dress as she crosses her legs. I turn my head away from Violet to see if he'll notice.

"Don't let her out of your sight," he says, slapping the seat. "No telling what she'll do."

Violet pushes hair from her face. "Wonderful way to treat your navigator."

She smells like a baseball field, reminding me of the day I ran away with Jamie. We'd found this baseball field nobody had played on since before The Burn. The field was overgrown with dandelions and first base had been gnawed by roaming dogs. We found a ragged baseball and tossed it around till the leather fell off and the yarn inside looked clawed at. Jamie said I'd find a cats-eye marble in the center under all the yarn, so that night, I unspooled the baseball while he slept in outfield. What I really found was an ugly little ball, tar-black and smooth as a stone.

The headlights outline a shack on the shore of Green River, not too far from the orphanage. Its tin roof is dark with rust. Water laps against the pilings, and the windows don't have screens.

"This is it." Violet turns and looks me in the eye. "Kid, will you loosen up and quit staring at me already?"

"No can do," I say, grinning.

As we make our way toward the shack, I notice that it lists toward the river. I wonder if it'll even support our weight. We knock on the door, but there's no answer. It's unlocked, so Jamie lets himself in, and I nudge Violet forward and follow her inside as well. The walls are decorated with black and white photographs of Confederate soldiers trying to look tough in their uniforms. One of the soldiers is covered with measles.

One face stands out among the rest. It's Jefferson Davis.

"I guess that confirms it," I say. It's kind of a question and kind of a statement. "These are Bottlecap's kin."

"That's a good assumption, considering that this is probably the only house outside of the South with pictures of a bunch of Confederates hanging on the walls," Jamie says, twisting his lithe, muscular frame to look at all the pictures along the wall. "Way to use your head, Kid."

"Thanks," I say, gazing hard at Jamie.

Violet crosses her arms. "Would you two get a room already?"

We find Bottlecap Murphy in the kitchen, and my fears about the house's stability are alleviated. The man's at least four hundred pounds, flat on his back in barbershop-striped shorts, dead as a doorpost. Pills are scattered around, a green bottle upturned next to his face. Over his head hangs a picture of him shaking hands with Barning's mayor. The picture looks like it was taken at the Daguerreotypes Den, a shop that opened next door to the B.W. General Store a couple of years back. I know the place well because I convinced Jamie to take a picture with me there just before we got involved with the bank robbery.

"Where the heck did this guy get enough pills to overdose?" I ask over Violet's shoulder.

"This bottle is old. Easily pre-Burn stuff," Jamie says.

Violet drops to her knees and crawls around, picking up the scattered pills. "These'll fetch a good price."

"Maybe he was doing what Violet's planning with those," I reply to Jamie.

"He wasn't selling them," Jamie says, fishing around in the man's mouth. "He was taking them himself. How he got them doesn't matter. It's what happened after he did."

"He took too many at once," I say.

"Nope," Jamie says, pulling a cap to a pill bottle from the back of the man's throat.

"He opened the bottle with his teeth," Violet says.

I lift one of my eyebrows. "You're a regular gumshoe, Violet."

"I'll be damned," Jamie says. "Kind of ironic if you ask me."

"Guess we can update this in the journal," I say.

"What're you talking about?" Violet asks. "What journal?"

"Fetch us a shovel," Jamie says to me, "and do something with her while you're at it."

I lead Violet along the shore to Bottlecap Murphy's shed, a tin A-frame on stilts so rotten a seagull could push it over. But it'll hold Violet long enough for Jamie to satisfy his hunch about Confederate gold, then I'll convince him to kick her to the curb.

"You going to kill me?" Violet asks, climbing the steps to the shed. Her red hair shines in the moonlight.

I laugh. "Jamie and me ain't the killing types."

"You may not be," she says.

Before I can say another word, she spin-kicks me in the gut, and I stumble into sand. She grabs me, pulls me to my feet, and puts me in a sleeper hold.

I raise my hands and mumble. "Let me go."

"Gladly." She drags me up the steps and shoves me into the shed.

The inside reeks of ripened fish, and a fishing knife is lodged between the floorboards.

"Why're you doing this?" I ask between coughs.

"Same reason as you." She snatches the shovel from beside the shed door and backs out. "Neither of us is who we seem to be." I run at her, but she slams the door and locks it before I can stop her.

Six months ago, I got locked in this old walk-in freezer that my daddy used to cure meat. Daddy ran a butchery from the house. The freezer didn't work, of course, and it was all beat up and smelled like spoiled jerky. Daddy had shoved me in there because he got pissed off that I hadn't done my chores. He shut the door behind him, said he'd leave me to think about my actions, and then went out to make a delivery.

Although the freezer wasn't functional, it was still cold in there because it was February in Vermont. Instead of doing my chores around the homestead, I'd trudged through the snow to the old junkyard where I liked to hang out and clear my head. It had a bunch of ancient cars and tractors and household junk from way before The Burn.

The snow had made my pant legs damp, and my ankles were freezing. Hiding my face against the aluminum wall, I felt isolated and out of breath. It was Jamie who finally saved me, and that's how we met.

The door swung open, and Jamie's lean frame was silhouetted by the daylight behind him. He'd been skulking around our homestead for days, stealing cheap cuts of meat. Although I'd seen his campfire flickering in the cow field three nights in a row, I hadn't yet made his acquaintance.

My teeth chattered. "Daddy and me were playing a game."

Jamie dragged me into a patch of frozen grass. "That's some kind of game," he said. "Your daddy plumb forgot about you." He helped me out and gave me his coat. "What should I call you?" he asked.

"Billy the Kid," I said, joking. I liked to pretend I was somebody, that people would actually notice me. I had this picture book of Old West outlaws, and The Kid was my favorite. Nobody crossed him, that was for sure.

Jamie took me back to his camp. Sitting beside the campfire, Jamie told me all these stories he knew from the Civil War. He said he liked to think about that time period because it reminded him that things were always shitty and people always scraped to survive, even before The Burn and The Collapse.

"It's kind of crazy, but now it's like we're living the way people did back then," he said.

We talked about our family histories and realized that our parents were both from the same neck of the woods. Jamie's dad was from Mississippi, and my mom and dad came from Alabama—back before The Burn.

As I understand it, after the solar flares hit, things went downhill quick. Somehow, word spread to our parents about folks making a new life in Vermont. Green mountains sure sounded better than baking under the furious sun in the South, and so they made the journey with groups of other families. This was before Jamie and me were ever born.

"I may have grown up in Barning, but I won't say my heart really belongs here," Jamie said. "Not that it matters much anyway. There's nowhere else to go unless you got connections and good shit to trade along the way. As it happens, I have neither of those things."

"Well," I said, sighing. "What we do have is each other."

Jamie slapped my shoulder. "You're all right, Kid."

As we shared a hunk of smoked jerky he'd stolen from my daddy, Jamie confided in me about how his own father used to knock him around. Then he told me about his epiphany.

"I'm bound to die of a broken heart," he said. "I had a vision this one time as my pops smashed my skull in. Broken heart. I'm telling you. That's just the way it's gonna be."

The fire spit and hissed. And Jamie, he was looking at me.

Trapped in the shed at Bottlecap Murphy's place, I sweat bullets and my t-shirt sticks to my chest. I search for loose spots in the tin walls and even threw myself against the door. The only thing this accomplishes is to hurt my shoulder. I have flashbacks to my time in my daddy's freezer.

I'm all alone and the walls feel like they're closing in on me. When I feel like this, like when I was locked in the freezer, I ball my fists like a toddler pitching a fit, close my eyes, and hide my face. My brain runs wide open. Last time I was trapped, Jamie came for me. Then I was able to return the favor when I got him out of harm's way during the bank robbery. We owe our lives to each other.

I tilt my head back and breathe—just breathe—and then open my eyes. Staring up at the rafters, I see a box perched on a rafter and the top of the wall in the far corner. The box is made out of dark, old wood, and it looks like nothing special. I almost don't spot it because it's recessed into the shadows.

Curiosity possesses me, and I shimmy up between the exposed studs and grab hold of the rafter and pull myself up there. I kick the box, and it's really heavy and probably hasn't been moved in years. But with a couple more well-placed kicks, the box falls to the floor and breaks open.

When I jump down, I don't believe my eyes. It's gold. Bricks of gold. The Great Seal of the Confederacy is stamped into them, which I recognize due to all the times Jamie has described it to me. When I'm trying to fall asleep at night, he has this habit of rambling on with all the facts he knows about history. On the seal, Jefferson Davis glares from his steed, sword holstered against his hip. The inscription reads: *Deo Vindice.*

God will vindicate.

Stepping back in surprise, I trip and land flat on my back. The handle of the fishing knife jabs into my spine. I holler and roll, and that's when I notice that one of the floorboards is loose. I use the knife to pry the board up, and then I climb out, landing in the shallow area of the river underneath the shed. Sloshing through the cool water, I spot a trench along the shoreline. Bottlecap must have been trying to trap fish.

I snatch open the side door of Bottlecap's house, which leads into the kitchen. The cabinets are open, plates shattered, drawers overturned. The table's propped against the sink, and the wall paneling is dotted with fist holes. Poor Bottlecap's been rolled on his stomach, his right arm pointing to the window. I follow his direction.

I step over busted pictures and see Jamie and Violet outside the window, illuminated by the radiant moonlight. They lean on the Plymouth's rear bumper, surrounded by shovel holes. Jamie's shirtless, and Violet's blouse sticks to her in the heat. She's sewing up his bullet wound.

I stand next to the windowsill, out of sight, and listen.

"How'd you find out about Murphy anyway?" Violet asks, knotting the thread. She cuts off the excess with Jamie's pocketknife and then hands the knife back to him.

Jamie winces as he puts the knife back in the front pocket of his jeans. "Want to know a secret?"

Violet tilts her head. "What kind of secret?"

Jamie pulls Bones' journal from the trunk and hands it to Violet.

Violet chews her lip. "I gotta read the whole thing?"

"Just the first and last page."

"Why?"

"Just do it."

She squints at the names.

"What's written there?" Jamie asks, looking on.

"Can't you read?" Violet says.

Jamie scoffs. "Just tell me."

Violet stutters, and her face drops. "Bottlecap Murphy's name is in here."

Jamie nods. "He's the last one who could've inherited the Confederate president's gold."

"You can't seriously believe that."

"I do believe it," Jamie says, closing the journal and tossing it back in the trunk. "And I believe something else too."

"Oh yeah?" Violet asks, stepping closer to Jamie. "What's that?"

Jamie grins, his one crooked tooth making him look like a devil. "I believe that the hunt led me to you for a reason."

"Are you saying what I think you're saying?" Violet asks.

"Yep." Jamie pulls her close. "For better or worse, we're meant to be together."

Next thing I know, they're kissing. And I mean really kissing—not like a friendly peck or anything. They keep on until they're halfway in the trunk. Violet wraps her legs around Jamie's waist. All alone and out of breath, I ball my fists and hide in the corner.

And that's when I notice that Bottlecap owns a telephone. I look up at the picture of him and the mayor. Bottlecap had friends in high places to get a line ran out here. I pick up the receiver, close my eyes, and dial number four.

The bank robbery two days ago was my first time holding a gun. The oak stock was heavier than I expected as I hoisted it like a marine cadet. I felt cold to my core, and I knew that was how a man should feel with a weapon in his hand.

Jamie frowned. "It's only got birdshot in it. It's all I could trade for—the bastard at the general store wouldn't come down on his price."

"What should I do?" I asked.

"Just back me up if things get crazy," Jamie said, spinning the loaded chamber of his six-shooter.

I sighted down the shotgun, accidentally tracking the barrel across Jamie's chest.

"Fuck! Be careful," he scolded, pushing the barrel toward the exterior door. "Don't want nobody getting hurt, especially me."

I gulped. "Sorry."

We stood in the foyer for another second, and then Jamie kicked open the door that led inside the main lobby of the bank. Across the lobby, Ronnie Younger was busy harassing the two clerks with a hunting rifle. His hair glared red, contrasting with his camouflage coveralls. Ronnie came from a long line of bear hunters, and with the silver-embossed nose of his grandfather's antique rifle, it was clear that he meant business.

Three bank customers huddled under a big rough-lumber table in the middle of the room. A bald man in a tattered shirt sobbed. A young woman with soot-colored hair sorted her bronze coins into piles. The last customer, a wrinkled old man, sat in slack-jawed terror. One of the two clerks backed away from the counter, and Ronnie yelled at him to keep his hands up.

The other clerk didn't move. She was taller than me, young, and had a petite cuteness about her that flirted with fakeness. She had shoulder-length brunette hair and a face shaped like a Valentine heart. She looked at Ronnie with a mixture of admiration and disgust. Ronnie eyed her like he'd give chase.

"You secure the front door?" he asked Jamie.

Jamie pointed his revolver behind him. "You see anyone coming or going, dipshit?"

Ronnie grunted. "Don't need no surprises."

"I'm a man of my word," Jamie said. "Who's this pretty thing?"

"Violet," the clerk said. "My name is Violet, and I am not a thing, pretty or otherwise."

"Violet the banker," Jamie said, nodding. He hopped over the counter. "Here's what you're gonna to do, Violet the banker. You're gonna show us the Rebel gold."

Violet giggled. "Or what?"

Jamie pointed the six-shooter at her temple. "Or you'll get hurt real bad."

The gun barrel pressing a ring into her forehead, Violet laughed. At the same time, tears ran down her cheeks. "You think that scares me?"

Ronnie got antsy and kicked the counter. As Violet turned, I saw that the thick rouge on her cheeks covered a bruise.

"Open the vault," Jamie said.

Violet walked to the steel door far back behind the counter and spun the combination. I jumped the counter and followed Jamie inside the vault, while Ronnie kept watch just outside. The vault was cold and smelled like a library. I didn't trust Ronnie as far as I could throw him, and I shivered at the thought of somehow being locked inside the vault if he decided to double-cross us.

I'd never seen so much old-school money in my life. Bundles were arranged in neat pyramids. Bills from before The Burn, some even as much as a couple centuries old, sat there in perfect stacks.

"We're about to start circulating paper money again," Violet said. "We can't trade bronze and silver and gold forever. It just isn't practical. So, we're stock-piling all the bills we can to increase demand." She paused, taking in our confused looks. "You know, the more contained and restricted the bills are, the more people will want to get their hands on them."

"Exactly," I said, faking both understanding and interest.

"Where's all the gold?" Jamie asked, pushing over a pyramid of bills. "Your source lied, Ronnie."

As unreliable a lookout as there ever was, Ronnie heard his name and stepped inside the vault with us. He looked around and grimaced. "There's a little here," he said, picking up one of several bags of gold ingots from beside the stacks of bills. He handed the bag to me, and I tied the drawstring to my belt buckle.

"That ain't what we came for," Jamie said. "I want the priceless Confederate gold you told me was here."

Ronnie shook his head. "There's plenty of cash here to make up for that," he said, stuffing a handful of bills in Jamie's shirt pocket.

"These bills ain't worth shit!" Jamie snatched the paper money out and threw it on the ground.

"Not yet," Ronnie said. "But they will be."

"We came for the gold," Jamie growled.

Ronnie shoved Jamie. "Screw the gold!"

Caught off guard, Jamie stumbled back. As he tried to regain his balance, Violet dove on top of him and wrestled the revolver from his grip.

I prepared to fire my shotgun.

"You'll hit me too," Jamie said. "That birdshot will spray everywhere."

"That's right," Violet said, pointing the six-shooter at Jamie's chest. "Now, lower that gun."

I did as she commanded.

"Empty your shells," Violet said to me. "And throw the gun on the floor."

I did as she asked.

"Good. Now you both better start walking."

Jamie and me walked with our hands up back into the main foyer.

"Now then, I'll give you a count of five to get gone," Violet said with a smirk.

The two of us broke into a run. Violet counted to three, and then a shot echoed. The bullet clipped through Jamie's shoulder just as he unlocked the exterior door. I grabbed Jamie and pulled him outside.

Before the door swung shut, I got one last glimpse of the scene inside. I saw Violet drop her pistol, appearing startled. Beside her, Ronnie Younger's rifle smoked. He had a treacherous look in his eye.

"You okay?" I asked.

He looked down at the wound, then gave me a knowing smile. "Looks like I escaped my fate after all."

I exhaled. "What now?"

"If the gold ain't here, then somebody else in this town has to have it," Jamie said, clutching his bloody shoulder. "In the meantime, we need to get moving and let things cool off."

I helped him to his feet. "I know of a junkyard where we might can salvage a ride."

⊙≈≈≋

Dew has settled on the windowsill in Bottlecap Murphy's kitchen, and the stars are glowing. After seeing Jamie and Violet going at it, I'd gotten so riled up that I got tired and nodded off for a few minutes on the floor. Bottlecap's corpse stares at me as I shake off the grogginess, dust my boots, and make for the door.

The business end of Ronnie Younger's rifle touches my nose, and I stop cold.

"Watch your step, Kid," Ronnie says, a grin dimpling his freckled cheeks. "Wouldn't want you getting shot."

Jamie's on his knees beside the Plymouth, hands tied in front of him. He's dusty, shirtless, and the stitching on his shoulder is torn open. Blood stains his bare chest. He has cold, dark eyes.

"What do you want, Ronnie?" I ask.

"You know why I'm here," Ronnie says.

"You came for the gold," I say.

"Sure as sugar," Ronnie says, slicking his hair. "Now get on your knees, outlaw. Over there with your partner."

"Hope it was worth it," I whisper to Jamie as I kneel next to him.

He cuts me a tired look. "He ain't gonna kill us."

"Just hurt us real bad," I say.

"Look, Kid," Jamie snaps, then hushes his tone. "Sorry I forgot about you."

"Shut your mouths," Ronnie shouts.

Ronnie turns his back, and Jamie springs up and shoulder-checks him. They tussle in the dirt, the long rifle wedged between them. Ronnie punches Jamie's shoulder. Jamie hollers, rolls on top of Ronnie, and uses his tied hands to pop Ronnie square in the face.

I pull off one of my boots and rear back to throw it. Before I can, shotgun pellets puff in the sand next to me.

"Next time, I don't mean to miss," Violet says from behind me.

"Thought you were sleeping in the car," Jamie says, eying her.

"The seats aren't comfortable," she replies.

I clear my throat, nodding at Ronnie. "I guess he's still your partner."

"That's right," she says, pulling Ronnie up. She flashes a smile at Jamie. "Good job figuring out that journal. You're a regular Einstein."

Jamie snorts. He sifts a fistful of dirt through his fingers.

"Too bad you couldn't find where Bottlecap hid his family's gold."

"Yeah, that's too bad," Jamie says. "Ain't that right, Kid?"

"Yep," I say. "A real shame."

As Violet and Ronnie turn to gaze at one another, Jamie flings sand at them. The sand pelts Ronnie in the eyes. While that is going on, I pitch my boot at Violet, and the wooden sole hits her in the temple.

Jamie and me break for the Plymouth, jump inside, and Jamie cranks it up. He slams the jalopy in reverse. As we spin around, the solar panels rattle on top. Jamie throws the gear in drive and guns it, while Ronnie fires blindly at us. The shot cracks a spiderweb in the windshield. "We lost this battle," Jamie says, stomping the gas, "but we ain't losing the war."

It was Sheriff Reginald who I'd called from Bottlecap's telephone before Ronnie showed up. The receiver vibrated against my ear, and Sheriff's voice came through in waves. All I could think about was Jamie and Violet wallowing in the Plymouth. My hand shook, but I tried to sound tough and not nervous.

"Sheriff's office." The man sounded like he was at the end of his shift and maybe the end of his rope. "Who's speaking?"

I agitated my voice. "You know damn well who's speaking, copper."

"Is this Billy the Kid?"

"Momma named me Hart," I said, "but you can take your pick of what you want to call me."

I heard paper crinkling. I imagined the sheriff digging under the latest issue of the *Barning News Record* for his notepad.

"I bet you could use another lead on that bank robbery," I said.

The sheriff chuckled. "Ready to turn yourself in?"

"You'll have to settle for another bone for the chase," I said. "But a bigger one this time."

The sheriff grunted. "Make it worth my time, kiddo."

"Icebox Creek. Up the shore you'll find a gravesite. One of our gang turned snake some time ago," I said, lying about Bones. "My partner dealt him a bad hand, but I never wanted to hurt anybody."

"You're in over your head, son," the sheriff said. "Let me help you."

"There's no helping me," I said, glancing out the window at Jamie and Violet making out. "I'm bound to die of a broken heart, just like my partner. Destiny is destiny, and there's no way around it."

"That's crazy talk," the sheriff replied.

I watched as Jamie unbuttoned Violet's blouse.

"*Deo vindice*," I said and hung up.

The day of Jamie's deliverance, I'm his passenger. I'm not nervous. It's just him and me, and that's the way it's supposed to be.

The glass in the floorboard is rough against my bare soles. Jamie hangs his arm out to touch the burning sky, a gob of tobacco in his mouth. Bones' journal rests between us. Cool air howls through the busted window, whipping curious circles that flutter the journal's pages.

An elm tree emerges from the darkness, its largest branch dipping over the road. Jamie tells me that's where the Union tied a hanging rope to deal with former Rebels who'd escaped north.

"Confederates never retreated, they just regrouped to fight again some other day," Jamie says.

"Even when they were outnumbered?" I ask.

"Even a hundred to one." He squares his shoulders and grips the steering wheel. "Even long after the war was over."

We turn down a trail, and the spare tire rattles as the Plymouth's back end fishtails. An incoming solar flare sparkles against the wind-shield, painting Jamie's face orange and red.

We head toward the creek where the rest of our gold bullion is stashed next to Bones' skeletal remains. Jamie's plan is to come back for our remaining ingots and then leave Barning for good. Word has it Violet and Ronnie are headed out West, and Jamie means to track them down.

"Shit," Jamie says, spotting a line of police carriages blocking the creek. They're positioned at the base of a steep hill, and Jamie perches the Plymouth at the top, presses the brake, and revs the engine. The car's weighty frame shakes, eager to plunge downward. Jamie grips the steering wheel and narrows his eyes. I taste blood.

One thing I know about Jamie is, he retreats like a true Rebel.

"We ain't gonna live forever," I say.

Sheriff Reginald stands beside the middle carriage, screaming mayday through a bullhorn. The horses neigh and thump their hooves as Jamie stomps the gas.

"Told you we were blood brothers," he says, not watching the road.

We clasp hands. And Jamie, he's looking at me.

Flesh, Wood, and Bone

Chloe Viner

I have returned to the time
before apples had brand names
and chickens had cages

I have hung by a thread
of hope and not hung
like my lover
before me

in the summer of my silence
dry wood cracked into splinters
like an elderly man's knuckles
left to the shattering
pain of the mundane
yet somehow the sun
rises the same

I taste your absence in
whispers and shouts
basements and attics
sweep cobwebs aside
it's all just
flesh and wood and bone

Tompkins Ventura

Richard Squires

Mama was dying, which was impossible. My mama was invincible.

"I'm afraid your mama isn't invincible at all," Dr. Healy said, then picked a rust-scab from his stethoscope and sent it flurrying to the floor. "She's caught a bad infection and will undoubtedly die if she doesn't get antibiotics right quick."

That was hard to buy. Mama could be in a room with the toughest sons a' bitches you've ever seen, and she was still the least likely to die. I'm serious. One time she was bitten by a rattler, a big boy. Everyone thought she'd die, but she sweated the poison right out. One year at the shindig on Solar Flare Day, an ember popped from the bonfire onto Mama's lap and lit up the bouquet I'd made her of yellowed newspaper. She was so deep in a moonshine stupor that the fire crawling up her belly didn't even wake her. She's lucky Sherriff Bets dumped the vat of bug juice on her. Dr. Healy worked all the next day cutting away the denim and cotton singed to her skin, Mama's only pain relief whiskey and wisecracks.

And there was the time the varmint Wesley Stiel shot her right in the heart. I saw it myself about half my life ago—I should be turning thirteen real soon, I think. Stiel's the one who last saw my Daddy. They'd gone beyond the walls out into Crazyland two months earlier, and Stiel had returned alone. He started spinning some yarn about how he and Daddy were on the cusp of saving the world until Daddy had gotten lost in some hole in a rock that he surmised was a portal to another dimension—silly stuff that Mama wasn't having. "You're a liar," she said. "You're yella." Her face was red as a flare she was so mad, her lips all dry and sticking up to her gums. Sherriff Bets, who was Daddy's best friend, was crowding Stiel and making him nervous.

Well, after more than an hour of interrogation, the pressure became such that Stiel pulled a tiny pistol from his ankle holster and popped one in Mama's chest. I remember it so well: the small gun sounded more like a whip than a bullet shot. Everything was quiet for a moment as Mama poked her finger through the hole in her shirts and pulled it out bloody.

"Loretta," Stiel said, his voice trembling, "I didn't mean to..."

Mama's hand came across with such force that her nails dug enough skin off his throat to expose arteries, or tissue, or whatever it was. It might've been his esophagus staring at me all aquiver. He turned a sick greeny-white, and when he swallowed, it was like opening a dam from which the blood poured out, painting his chest and the floor all red.

You shouldn't lie to Mama, especially about Daddy. You shouldn't shoot her, neither.

Dr. Healy observed Mama at the infirmary for a couple weeks, then said, "Well, Loretta, you sure are hard to kill. I recommend leaving that bullet right where it is for now."

So there you have it: you can't kill Mama. Only she was in a bad way, and I was starting to worry.

Mama is a huge hunk of love, and that tends to get her in trouble. The predicament I want to tell you about started with a virus that swooped into Barning a few weeks earlier and took with it like fifty souls. Then Drunk Isiah and Dave, Barning's gravediggers, got tired I guess and ditched work for the Silver Blade Saloon while a pile of twenty bodies or so stunk up the yard. The Silver Blade's got poison juice and naked ladies, so people who go in tend to stay a while. I don't see what all the fuss is.

The schoolhouse ain't far from the Barning graveyard, just down the tracks. One day Mama swears she can practically see the rotting stink and diseased skeeters floating off the pile of bodies and into the upstairs schoolhouse window where I sit for the few days we got to go learn something every week. "Well, Tommy-tom-Tompkins Square Park Eldridge Ventura," she said, "an epiphany slugged me right in my gut." And, by the way, Mama's got a solid gut.

She gets this brilliant idea to make sure the job gets done so her precious little boy—I'm nearly a man, actually—don't catch sick. "Them bodies gotta get buried," she said, "and I'm gonna see to it." Well, that toxic mist she imagined floating up through my classroom window, she sucked it right in.

"Tom," Dr. Healy said, "I'm sorry, son, but there's nothing here that will do your mama any good. We already used up everything we had a few weeks back. Your Ma's a good woman, a big, big heart. I can try to make her more comfortable."

Comfortable? Mama never needed no comfort. Since Dr. Healy couldn't help, I had to go see someone Mama never wanted me mixing with: Numi, this strange lady who likes to poison herself. She says it makes her laugh. Says it makes her wise too. And plenty of people like to buy poison from her, but none of them seem to get any wiser. Numi lives in a rickety trailer she calls an apothecary at the ass-end of town.

Bone-skinny and dressed like a rainbow, she reminds me of one of them peacocks I seen in the old pictures. She got nice big hair she fills with ribbons and beads. The sky was dark gray and thundering when I knocked on Numi's trailer. When she finally answered the door, I could see she'd been deep asleep. Her eyes were little slits, and her hair was teased in the back like tumbleweed.

"I know why you've come to me, Tompkins."

I sat in her rocking chair, and she handed me a small cup of tea.

"Then you'll help Mama? I'll pay you back, you know I will."

"I know, Tompkins. You're a man of your word. Like your daddy. But I've got nothing for her. I'd help you, honest, if I could."

I looked at her shelves. They teemed with containers and bags and scales. Her walls were lined with cabinets, all locked up.

"I got a lot of stuff here," she said. "But none can help your mama." To hold back tears, I gulped the rest of the tea. Then I stood.

"Numi," I said, "forgive me, but I'm about to give you some lip. 'Cause there ain't gonna be nothing for you to say to me ever again unless you open all them cabinets and make a concoction. My mama's in the hospital, and she's big with love but small with life." I felt a little sick and cleared my throat. "Dr. Healy can't do nothing normal, so it's down to you to do something weird. You comprehend me, Missus?"

Well, I think Numi got the message. Her hands trembled as she unlocked a cabinet, grabbed one of those old plastic bags you can seal up, and dumped in some needles and powder. She plopped the bag on my lap.

"This'll save Mama?"

"No. That'd kill your mama pretty quick."

I didn't understand.

"But that'll buy you what you need to save your mama."

"From a medicine man? Like you?"

"You just tell him Numi sent you." I wanted to hug her. "But Tompkins, it's dangerous. You'll die out there. It'll be even worse for your mama if she loses you too. Besides, she won't allow you to go. I know it."

"I ain't afraid of Mama," I said, and then remembered that everybody's afraid of Mama. I swiped dust from my hair and watched it sink to the floor. "And I ain't afraid of no adventure."

I checked in on Mama. It was dim in the hospital, just a few candles flickering shadows over the walls and gurneys. Mama was asleep. Red splotched her pale face. Her big shape was funny, like her organs and fluids were sinking into the cot. I sat with her a while. Then I kissed her forehead.

I stopped home for some gear, then headed down Court Street. The sun was falling back in the woods, sparkling off Green River like a cloud of fireflies. I stopped, wanting to feel that Barning warmth on my face, wanting to look and take it in so completely it would be like a picture I was carrying in my pocket, in case I wanted to pull it out and look at it on my travels. In case I was feeling sad and lonely, or I couldn't get back so quick.

Then I booked it to one of the old mineshaft entrances. That's where I hid my ol' bicycle. It had been my daddy's, and his daddy's before him. Mama said I should never tell nobody about it, that it was a valuable item, a mountain bike, built to last all those years ago. Mama had helped me hide the bike real good across two beams above the entrance. I pulled it out and headed over to the west gate. Whoever was supposed to be on watch duty had probably slipped over to the saloon for a nip. No surprise. So I slid on out.

Dark was coming on. Dust whipped in the torrential wind. I pulled on my black ski mask, set my goggles over my eyes, zipped up my parka, slipped on my padded and fingerless gloves, tightened my pack straps, and hit it. The wind at my back helped me ride faster than I'd ever ridden before.

The world beyond Barning's walls was more pavement, cracks, and holes than I'd imagined. I was cruising along, the wind throwing debris at my back, when I hit a ditch, flipped off my bike, and landed on my shoulder. I slowed down after that. I had to stop and carry my bike over a lot of fallen trees, but the smaller ones had rotted enough where I could roll over them. Autos littered the place. I weaved through. A couple times they were bunched so thickly I had to climb over. Rust ate away at them like a fungus. I had to be careful I didn't cut myself. That's the kinda wound that might never close up. Vines strangled the autos, pulled them into the ground. Because of the pressure, wheels had caved under.

There was a lot of burnt stuff, and it smelled moldy. Many of the towns I rode through had been decimated in The Burn decades ago. You could tell they'd been built a lot earlier than Barning of older, weaker materials, and when the solar flares hit, there'd been a spark that grew into a mean wall of fire and just rolled through everything. Other towns were stone and brick, some of the structures still standing, lotsa caved-in roofs.

There were a bunch of uphills, little mountains, but the uphill work was rewarded with downhill cruising. I made really good distance by the time the sun was rising. It was perfect, because I was looking for Route 4 to turn toward ol' Rutland, and just when it was light enough, there was the sign, still standing. A little saggy and grimy, but alive. I'd found Route 4 sooner than I'd expected.

A short way down, I heard a group of men up ahead. Sounded like they were fighting. Then some of them would laugh. Then they'd be screaming again. I kept my distance. I could hear a couple horses clopping on the road, and creaky wooden carriage wheels, so I didn't get no closer or farther. But then, as I came around a bend, I saw a man lying in the road. At first, I thought maybe it was Daddy.

I crouched where he couldn't see me. Blood pumped from a gash in his forehead and slicked his hair. It looked like he was breathing just a little. It was easy to see this wasn't a big, blond-haired man with monster hands. I was relieved I hadn't found my daddy like this. Then I thought maybe those fellers on the carriage were too drunk to realize they'd lost a guy, and they would come back looking for him.

Besides, I was tired. There was a yellow bus, a school bus they're called. We got one of them back in Barning. They got lots of cushy benches to choose from if you wanna lie down. But this bus was tilted, and I didn't wanna keep sliding one way when trying to get some sleep. So I checked down the winding dirt drive behind the bus.

A big metal tower, like what they used to use for electricity, was bent over. It made a tunnel. I rode through and soon came to a wooden house with a windmill still standing behind it. Crude wooden crosses poked from the dirt in the yard. A telephone pole leaning against the house had caved one end of the roof. Black wires sagged. The rest of the roof was full of holes where nail-studded planks had popped out and warped.

But it didn't smell too bad. I carried the bike up the porch steps, sure to walk gingerly. Didn't want to step on a bad plank and fall through. I found an old couch that'd do the job, and I slept.

I woke near dusk, ate some granola and jerky, then headed back out. That man was still there in the road, and when I passed him, his eyes opened. "Hey," he rasped. I didn't want no part of him. "Help me." What could I do? I was on a mission for Mama, and that was that. "I cracked my skull," he said. I just shook my head. "My brain's leaking out, you little bastard." He coughed, then clenched his eyes. I watched his face register a whole progression of pain. "Put me down, at least."

I suppose I might've looked for a piece of wood with a nail sticking through it and whacked him in the head a few times. But thinking about it made me nervous. I'd never get it out of my memory. "Sorry," I said, and pushed on my pedals.

I rode a while more, and finally when the moon was at its highest, I found what I'd been looking for: *Kill Creek Quarry and Mine*. Numi said there'd be a sign, and there it was. So I turned down a dirt road and cruised a while until the trees opened to a large area with piles of broken rock and dirt. Dust hung in the air like fog. Old construction vehicles littered the place, big things with claws and shovels. This was the biggest and one of the oldest mines in Vermont, Numi'd told me. They used to pull out a lot of granite and marble. The mine shafts, she said, went real deep into the earth, and there was a whole maze of them, like a hundred or so. "Be careful you don't get lost in there," she said, "or you'll meet your end."

I rode down all these different levels of packed stone—like a giant staircase—to the mine opening, left my bike, and entered the darkness. The cave was vast and cold. Wind hummed and whipped my face. Water dripped somewhere and echoed. So many tunnels led who-knows-where. But one of the tunnels was a little bigger than the others. The sound of the wind was lower, as though it came from a deeper place. And it took my echo just a little longer to return. So I continued that way and found a long staircase that went further into the earth.

It was freezing at the bottom, dead-of-winter cold, and pitch black, but I wasn't afraid. I kept telling myself I was not afraid. Mama was relying on me. I kept on for a long while, slowly, softly, listening to the crunch of my footsteps, the wind, the swirling echo. I soon got used to the darkness and fell into a rhythm.

I wondered if it was my imagination or was the tunnel getting narrower and warmer. Then I tripped, and it wasn't over stone. I felt around and found something warm, rubbery, and long, like a big anaconda. It scared the bejeezus out of me. But when it didn't move, I gained the courage to touch it again. It wasn't no snake, yet it seemed alive because it buzzed at a real low level. When I touched it, I could hear it hum. It felt like a big electrical cord, not that I'd ever seen a working one.

It wouldn't budge. I followed it down the path until it turned and plunged right into the earth. This was the strangest thing. I scooped away stone and dug down. I just had to see where this cord led. The further down I dug, the louder the buzzing and the warmer the space. I kept on for a while until finally I hit the bottom. It wasn't rock or dirt, but a plank of wood. When I knocked, it sounded hollow underneath. I searched for an edge, but no luck. So I smashed it with my heel. I smashed it again and again, and finally the plank cracked.

And then the weirdest thing: this warm white light, bright as the sun, shot up like a spear. My heart pounded in my chest like a skittish weasel trying to flee a predator. I took some deep breaths and pictured Green River to calm myself, looking in my mind at the sunlight skimming off the water and feeling the warmth on my face. Then I put my eye to the crack. It was a moment before I could see anything, but when I could see, I was completely baffled. The character of the air down there in this big bright open space—and I don't mean the air you breathe, I mean the substance of the territory between the cliffs, the big metal structures, what looked like an elevated train track, and other things I saw—was dizzying. Every inch or atom in my view had more contour to it, more depth and detail. It was so hard to comprehend, but just looking gave me the feeling of seeing past, present, and future all at once. Nothing was happening in this space I observed, and yet every inch of it seemed to be rolling. The longer I stared, the better my eyes adjusted, the more beautiful it was. It was like looking into another dimension. Like what the varmint Wesley Stiel had been blabbering about.

"Dad?" I hollered into the space. My voice echoed in a way I'd never heard before. It bounced off the cliff across the way, back past where I was poking my head out to a cliff behind me, then past me again, my voice zigzagging all around this wide-open land as though in a small empty room.

The doorway let out onto the top of a metal tower that looked easy to climb. I decided I was going in and started pulling at the plank to make a bigger opening when a deafening gunshot rang out back down the tunnel. Sparks ricocheted off the ceiling and walls, and chips of stone pelted me in my ass.

"459! Burglary!" A gravel voice rolled down the tunnel. He shot again and the gun nozzle flashed. "Intruder!" His voice discharged at me. "I got you pinned against the rock shaft of your own anus. Trespassing's punishable by death in these parts. Now I'm gonna give you three Mississippis or you ain't never gonna see daylight again."

"Don't shoot," I hollered, and quickly remembered I was on a mission for Mama. "Trent?" I pushed stones back over the portal and started toward him. "Numi sent me. I brought something for you." It felt like the wind was blowing my voice back at me. But I just kept talking, saying Numi's name over and over. When I was close, I said, "She told me to tell you it's alright. She heard you wishing for her."

"Numi?" He raised what he was pointing at me, which was a grade A military automatic, I'm sure of it. "No shit?"

"Honest, Sir."

"Come closer." He stopped me when I stood the length of two yellow buses from him. In the darkness I could only see his outline. His head looked funny, flat on top. "Well, okay," he said, and tossed me a bag. "Put it over your head." Then he guided me back out of the tunnel, spun me a few times so I'd lose my bearings, and pushed me down some other tunnel. I could hear him fiddling with locks and doors. Then it got bright. He pulled off the bag.

I couldn't believe it. He had a whole hideaway, and it was fancy-pants, too. This wasn't no medicine man. This was a doomsday man. Trent wore combat boots, a navy military uniform, pants with cargo pockets, a utility belt with a gun and bullet clips, knives and other things, and a vest with more supplies. But his face was lined like a palm and was the whitest white. Like he'd never seen the sun. His hair was white too, shock white. He'd buzzed it flat, but he really only had hair toward the back. I realized he was old. The oldest man I'd ever seen. You could tell he'd once been big and strong, a classic soldier type, but now he was wiry, a bit hunched. His eye sockets were deep and dark. Veins crawled his temples like worms. He scratched white whiskers beside his mean mouth.

"'Chu lookin' at, boy?"

His shelter lit up nice, and so far underground. I asked him how.

His mouth got a little less mean. "Ah, these are your classic bulbs," he said. "From way back when."

"But how do they work?"

"Oh, I wouldn't know that kind of thing. A filament, or something."

The furniture was old, the leather cracked, but it was comfortable and smelled nice. He offered me coffee and poured it from a fancy, see-through pot. And then I noticed this thing that looked like a big black window. He pushed a button, and there were people in it. They were real, only they were so clean. Everything was new. And there were shiny autos that actually worked. Another portal, I thought, but when I touched the window, it was closed. I asked Trent if I could go in, and he started laughing.

"What, you never heard of a television?"

Sure, I'd heard of it in the history book. And Old Man Rapella had mentioned it in his stories, but... "But how do you have the power for it?"

Trent changed. His hand jerked to his pistol grip. He realized it, then shoved his hand in his pocket. He closed the window black, grabbed me by my jacket, and jammed the zipper into my chin. His lips and the muscles under his eyes twitched. "What you want with my power?" His breath was impressive, minty. "You Barning fucks'll never understand. This is my daddy's legacy, and I'm sworn to it. You Sugarbush fucks. You Shelburne fucks. I'm sick a' you all thinking you know something and fuckin' up my peace treaties." He was excited, breathing on me. "I'll tell you one thing: there's a tunnel out there, and it's full of dead men." He unholstered his pistol, cocked it, then closed his eyes and pressed the metal to his face like it was a girl from the Silver Blade Saloon. "Dead men," he whispered, "fevered up for glittering things without even asking themselves why."

I was tired of fancy tunnel breath, so I decided to start crying. Try to coax some sympathy, steer our little meeting back on topic. I blabbered about how Mama was dying, I ain't got no daddy, and so forth.

He let go of me, thought about something a long moment, then pulled a stick out of some package—a cigarette, I realized, when he lit it. One of those ancient, manufactured types. He leaned his head and an elbow against the wall while he smoked and coughed. Maybe he was crying. I had to get going.

"I been down here probably fifty years," he said. "My daddy was ten or thereabouts when the shit collapsed. These mines were his. We was rich. He just knew the world was shit. This is what you get for being a survivor. All this. Nothin.' I been alone fifteen years. Just me and my TV. I seen everything five thousand times. All the shows, all the movies. Just makes you more lonely. Shit ain't real. It fucks with your head."

"Whyn't you try and find some people? They're out there, you know."

"Thing is, after I lost my daddy, my ma, and my sister, I did go out. Had me a woman. Child too. Little girl. But my woman took her. Couldn't stand it down here. With me. With what I dedicated my life to. It's bigger than us all."

"You didn't follow her?"

"How am I gonna go out there and protect the world down here at the same time?" The back of his neck was really hairy. "Besides," he lit another smoke, "you know how some people remind you of other people?" I didn't. "Even the made-up people in the TV, they all seem like somebody. I keep thinking, *If I could just forget*. But copper can't stand in for gold."

"Don't I know it."

He turned around then plopped into a chair. I told him why I'd come, how I needed an antibiotic, and I tried to lay it hard that if he helped me have more time with Mama, he'd prove Numi right that he was a good man.

His nostrils flared and his lips curled down. "Hell she did. Don't you come into my bunker and lie to me. She knew me when I was different. What'd she say? Better tell me true."

Well, she hadn't said much. The bunker was getting warm. "Nothing. She said you'd have what I need, and she gave me a package to pay you."

He looked at my pack. He was suddenly a different man, chewing on his lip. His mouth was wet, dribbling. "The thing about this world..." he said. His fingers were white where he clenched the chair arms. "...is that when you do something to somebody, you can disappear, never again look at what you done. But you still see it. Everywhere you look. Now I'm going to tell you something else 'cause I am an honest man. If what's in that bag ain't what I'm hoping it is, I'm gonna get real mad. Give it here."

My swallow sounded like a choking frog. "Well," I said, trying to make my voice low, a man's voice, "whatever it is, it can't be switched out for nothing now." I threw him the pack.

He opened it slow. Saliva dripped in. He pulled out my clothes and tossed them aside, pulled out my knife, my slingshot. Then he pulled out the plastic bag.

Craziness glazed his full moon eyes. Tears ran his cheeks. "I been lonely too long," he sang as he took off his vest and rolled up his sleeve. He pulled a rubber string from the bag and tied it around his arm, then scooped a little of that special powder into a spoon and held a match under it. While the stuff turned liquid, he mumbled, "Lil Numi knows me. This is what I call dying in heaven."

"Dying?" I asked. "Who said anything about dying?"

"I did, boy. This is it, my ticket. Veins been..." and he sang again, "...lonely too long. Yeah, lonely."

The needle sucked the stuff up. He shot it into his arm, sat back, and closed his eyes like he'd eaten the best supper ever.

"Trent, sir? Are you plannin' on dying?" He didn't respond, so I asked again.

"Next week or so." He scratched his neck. "My duty in this hell's about wrapped up."

"You wanna die so bad, whyn't you just off yourself?"

"Oh, this is good R and R, baby. It's worth the wait." He laughed. "You have no idea."

"But, what about the power?"

He opened his eyes. "Don't you talk about something you can't understand."

"So it is power? Is it electricity, for real?" I started thinking what electricity would mean for Mama, and the infirmary, and all the tools we'd be able to use to heal people. "We need it."

"It don't belong to us!" he snapped. "We can't just take it for our own purposes, understand?"

I didn't understand at all.

He cleared his throat. His skin was shiny, moist. "It ain't relevant anyway because I figured out how to seal the doorway off. Don't bother trying to come back for it. Won't be nothin' here."

"You're gonna kill our chance. That's what Daddy was after. Don't you want to save the world?"

He pulled his gun from the holster, laid it on his lap, and moved his thumb back and forth over the grip. "That's what I'm doing. I'm protecting their world from us. In the same breath, I'm protecting our world from them. You see, one of us is more dangerous than the other, and I don't want to find out who. My pop never shoulda' dug so deep into the earth." He closed his eyes. "Now it's time for you to get." He rotated the gun to point my way.

I swallowed. "I need the meds for my mama."

"Oh yeah." He stood and wobbled. "Get up." Under the couch cushions was a trunk. He searched his pants, then the vest across the room, and found the key. There were all kinds of supplies in there.

"Healthy stuff," he said. "I already did all the good shit." He pointed. He moved like he was under water. "I believe that's what you want. Take as much as you can carry."

I jammed my pack. He made me put the bag over my head again.

It was near dusk when I got outside.

"You tell Numi 'Hi' from me, would you? Tell her I'm...well...oh nothing. Just that I'm...I'm sorry, I guess, about the way things went down." He kicked a small stone.

I didn't want to leave yet. I had so many questions. But there was no point since he wasn't talking. And I had to get back to Mama.

The bag was heavy, but I made steady speed. I rode all night. The moonlight was generous. Sometime past the middle of the night, when the moon started dipping into the jagged branches, I came upon that guy in the road. His soft parts—his stomach, his throat—had been opened up and chewed at. I could see through a crack in his scalp to his brain. When the light started coming on, I got off the road at a farm with a silo that had no door. There was some dry hay in there. I slept a few hours.

I was feeling like my luck was just too darn good, and I got scared that if I traveled in the daylight I'd run into some rough company. But I was itching to get to Mama, so a few hours before dusk, I hit the road. And by midnight, I was knocking on Barning's west gate.

A few minutes later, it slid open. And there stood Big Sheriff Bets. And what'd she do to me? Lifted me off my bike, carried me in like I was a piece of firewood, and threw me to the dirt. "Dumb little boys ain't allowed out," she hollered, and hitched up her gun belt.

I'd never given her lip in my life. But I stood, clapped my dirty palms, and said, "Well I ain't a..."

But she slapped me. I don't remember falling. I was just on the ground again.

"Your mama's been crazy about you, keeping the whole town awake," she said.

"But I got medicine."

"Oh." She changed at that and put me on my feet. I followed her to the infirmary.

Mama was sweating something serious. Seemed she sweated off some of her weight. She was mumbling all kinds of gibberish, talking as though Daddy was there.

"What you got, Tommy?" Dr. Healy asked. I just handed him my pack, nervous that what I'd picked up was the wrong thing. He pulled out the package, flipped it over, read it. He looked at me.

"Well?"

"Yeah," Bets said. "What's the verdict?"

"You did good," Healy said.

Two days later, Mama was back to her senses. Half a day after that, she was sitting up slurping soup. I waited another whole day to tell her. We were sitting on the infirmary porch, Mama in the rocking chair. It was a crisp blue morning. I could smell the cold winter coming. Mama was gonna need a lot of firewood, but I didn't want her doing all the chopping. I'd have to talk to Bets before I left.

"My Tompkins," Mama said. "I can always tell when you thinkin' something you ain't saying."

My heart was beating fast. I pressed my palm to my chest. "I think," I said. "I think Wesley Stiel wasn't lying. I know where Daddy got stuck."

Mama stopped rocking. "Is that so?"

"I'm gonna bring him back."

"Tommy-Tom-Tom. You go on one adventure and you think you're a man. You wanna do something, boy, you still got to ask your mama."

I looked out at the sky again and thought how strange to know there was a sky of another color in some other place. Yeah, winter was coming.

"Mama?"

She grunted.

"Mind if I borrow your axe?"

Her head didn't move, but her eyes shifted to me.

"I should take your gun, too. That gonna be okay?"

Water, Walls, Wicked

Chloe Viner

A starfish knows the sea
child knows their home
singer knows the stage
there is so much beyond
water, walls, Wicked

An addict to the needle
a worker to the queen
we were never sure what
it was all for

No more
Eiffel Tower
Statue of Liberty
Boston Museum of Fine Art, Uffizi
hipsters buying fourth edition copies
of *To Kill a Mockingbird*
graduations, caps, claps, or diplomas

All of us soldiers in this war
no funerals
we buried so much more than
our dead
beyond the water, walls,
and Wicked.

Nightshade

Devin Gaither

1.

Equal parts blackberry leaf, valerian root, ground bone of dog, dried blood of vulture, chamomile.

Numi carefully poured the hot water through the mound of herbs and other... medicinals...collected in the strainer.

One boney hand reached out and slid the deep blue ceramic honey pot across the scratched kitchenette counter. It skittered unevenly, sticking here and there to the years of grime worked into the surface. She inspected the bottom of the vessel and sighed. The fine lines in its ceramic belly shone in the dim, flickering light. The thin, sticky coating at the bottom would yield just enough for these two cups tonight.

Her tea was not good; it wasn't meant to be good. However, it was efficient. Efficient enough that most of her customers were happy to choke it down, but the honey had more benefits than just sweetening the sometimes-bitter medicine. It loosened the tongue. Loosened the mind, too, she supposed. This small luxury acted as a sensory trigger of a different time, as Numi's mother used to say, a time before The Burn, when a dollop of honey in one's tea was a matter of course—now, it was something most individuals hadn't even thought of in years.

She scraped the bottom of the pot before sliding it back into its spot between the nearly empty jar of dried thistle and her coveted jar of fat drippings, which was also close to empty. Unlike other residents of Barning, she wouldn't pretend not to take pleasure in small things, in setting small indulgences aside for those days when the never-ending cycle of survival stretched infinity into the future ahead of her. Indulging in the warm, half-forgotten taste of life before the apocalypse from time-to-time was not the same thing as clutching to the bones of yesteryear's society with denial and fear.

She looked down the counter at the rest of her stock jars.

It had not escaped Numi's notice that all of the jars in her stock were more than half empty. It hadn't happened suddenly. She had felt the knot in her stomach grow as, gradually, the demand for her services outpaced the yield of her small, moonlit harvests. She knew there was no other course to be had, but it was difficult to fear something that would happen months, perhaps years down the road when the chance was likely that one would die at any moment. Such was the way of life in the decades after The Burn. But here she was. The years had passed, and she was now faced with the realization that the graveyard was beginning, like all of the other land in Barning, to go barren. The hot water slowly transformed as the amber inclusions of the steeping tea wound their way through the heart of the cup.

How many more cups of this tea would she be able to make, even without honey, before her stocks were depleted? Twenty? Surely no more than thirty, and that was, she reminded herself, precisely why she had to keep up her end of her...dark bargain. It wasn't much of a choice in the end, but that did not mean she slept easy over it. A bloody pact, such as she found herself in, rarely allowed one much sleep, both from moral dilemma and physical labor combined. Dark deeds were, she was surprised to find, quite a lot of work—largely thankless and dirty.

Numi arranged the mug of hot tea, a small helping of pomegranate seeds, and a ceramic disk of milk-water on the small tray she used for guests and customers. Milk-water would never pass for creamer, but Numi had found that if she mixed powdered milk with half the normal amount of water and added a small amount of ground, soaked nuts (when she could find them), it made a close enough approximation to bring some comfort to the soul. And most of the time, that is exactly what her customers were truly seeking—comfort to the soul. No one ever asked how it was she managed to grow fresh pomegranates in her fortuneteller's trailer at the edge of the graveyard, and honestly, she preferred it that way.

She carried the wooden tray to the small kitchenette booth. This was where she sat with most of her customers. Or were they patients? It was difficult to say...some came to her for healing and others for answers. These things were sometimes more alike than one might realize, and so Numi sold tinctures and Numi told fortunes and Numi, generally, did her best to help people living in impossible conditions.

Today, her patient was a young woman by the name of Shelly. She was draped over the small rectangular kitchenette table, slumped forward in the raggedy booth with her head resting in her basketed fingers. Numi sat down across from her and set about fixing Shelly's cup. With a steady hand she fished out the small particulates that had escaped her makeshift, handmade strainer.

Numi slid the cup of tea between Shelly's elbows, and the woman groaned as the scent hit her nose.

Shelly plucked the cup from the table and held it in front of her face, reveling in the strong scent. Numi's eye caught a pattern in the rising steam, and she watched the dancing tendrils as they curled in upon themselves, winding inward like snakes, eager to eat their own tails. Then suddenly they were gone, faster than she could put a name to them, and she was looking past the steam into the face of Shelly.

Here was someone who clearly felt trapped in this new world. Shelly was in genuine pain, Numi could see that much without a full examination. Originally, Numi had thought it could be a blood sickness. Then, she wondered if it could be her change, come on her early, like so many these days; but in the end, Numi realized the truth was much simpler and much more difficult to treat.

Shelly was tired. Physically and mentally, to be sure, but also emotionally—and perhaps most of all, spiritually. It was not quite depression, not quite consumption. If Numi hadn't paid attention to the stories of the times before The Burn, a time of medical science and oversaturated with certainty, she may have thought Shelly's body simply lacked the will to live. She knew better, of course. Somewhere, the formal education of science, health, and biology passed on from her mother was etched into her core. But those lessons were a lifetime ago, and this woman now sat in front of Numi, wasting away from nothing in particular, other than the conditions of the world.

Her condition was, perhaps, not worse than last time, but it was consistent. This was not someone seeking the high of some of Numi's medicinals, but it was, she thought, a person seeking escape from something, an escape from the endless tension that the woman carried in her body by just living, by keeping her family alive, and from constantly being in a state of vigilance. Numi could give her teas like this one for the physical aches, remedies to quiet the pains of a post-apocalyptic life. *As long as I still have the ingredients to make the teas*, she thought, glancing at the collection of half-empty jars before putting them once again from her mind. But she could not give her patient a treatment for the dread that sometimes took hold and turned itself into madness.

"It's near constant these days," Shelly said, setting the steaming mug down. She rubbed her hands across her face. Her hands sweat, leaving tracks in the dirt on her cheeks. She placed her fingers on the handle and rim of the cup, as though she could use the mug to steady herself. "A pressure behind my eyes and cheeks, but also like there's a band squeezing around the crown of my head."

"It is probably the air quality," Numi said in a gentle monotone, closely searching Shelly's face for less obvious symptoms. "It is drying to the membranes, and the water rationing is making it worse. You must make sure you're getting your full rations."

"I grew up here. I would have expected my body to have evolved by now," Shelly mumbled as she took a sip. She winced, but whether it was in response to the temperature of the water, the taste of the medicinal, or the pain in her head, Numi could not be sure.

"Evolution takes hundreds, thousands of generations," Numi said. "I'm afraid we have been thrust into an environment we were not bred for. You've been having nosebleeds."

"Many, over the last two weeks," Shelly said, absentmindedly touching her upper lip with her index finger. There were those who thought Numi possessed supernatural abilities. They called it "intuition" or "energy reading." Others saw her for what she was: simply shrewd and observant. Numi was able to shut out the strangeness of the world's current circumstances and see things in their most straightforward components.

Yes, Shelly's nostrils were raw and peeling, yet she did not seem to be producing mucus. She said she had been having pressure in her head and face, as well as near constant headaches.

Numi noticed that the woman's breathing was shallow and pained and the whites of her eyes were red and pink. "Let me get you some goldenrod and catnip to take home with you. I'll just be a moment."

2.

It's amazing, the variety of people you still saw in this strange world, Numi thought to herself. She weaved through the graveyard, past the monoliths and stones and plaques, toward the plot she sought. The grave of Ursa Rauth sat just to the west of an old weeping willow that stood like a wire skeleton against the putrid sky.

The world had become monochrome, beige and dry-hay cross-hatching across the horizon, stretching as far as the eye could see (which, in the permanent smog, wasn't very far). The sky was no longer blue, but a ruddy, hazy yellow. The people, however, were as colorful as ever. Numi had observed three kinds of people emerge from the smoldering ruins of the old world over the years. Three flavors of human crawling from the ashes, clawing their way through the corpse of a town that called itself Barning, Vermont.

First, there were the deniers. Those trying to hold on desperately to the stories they knew of the before-times. The ones attempting to resurrect a dead age forever beyond their reach, a world in which they might mean something. Shelly was one of these flavors of people. Over their last several conversations, Numi had learned that she still tried to observe birthdays and holidays. She acted like, any day now, the U.S. government would come together again to roll in and save them all. Shelly held onto a near-delirious hope that someday soon they would find out that there was still a central governing body somewhere in the former country, and that someone had better be ready to start up the neighborhood watch at a moment's notice.

The second type of person that Numi was accustomed to seeing were those touched by the Flare Madness. They wore the blank looks of someone who has been cast out of heaven and into an eternity of barely surviving. These people were easy to spot. They existed someplace else, lost in silent madness that only they could understand. This was the kind of person that Shelly could become if she wasn't careful. If she let herself be dragged down into a mute, disassociated hell of her own mind.

And then, lastly, were the fire walkers. Those thriving in this new world, those running head-first into fire and brimstone. The ones that were not afraid to walk through the fire, as it were, leaning into the post-apocalyptic world in both image and practice. They dressed the part, they accepted the world as it was, and they were determined to not just survive in it, but to embrace it. To some, it was a game, to others a mission, and to others still—those with something in their old lives they were running from—it was an answer to a terrible prayer.

Numi rounded the mugwort-covered grave marked with the name *Alexandra*, strode past three barren plots, and finally arrived alongside the goldenrod-covered grave of Ursa Rauth. It stood out against the surrounding landscape, a patch of aggressive green and yellow against the sickly, dry surroundings.

Indeed, Numi felt as though the people of Barning, Vermont, were more colorful than ever. No one existed casually in the apocalypse. Except, perhaps, Numi. Numi fit into the sepia landscape like she had been painted directly onto its canvas at its conception.

3.

Growing up in Barning, Numi had taken a liking to plants. She knew that before The Burn it was a trendy thing to at least have a passing knowledge of houseplants and to be able to show off one's green, aesthetic home. If she sat down and thought about it, she supposed she had also known, in the early days, that forest fires would normally make the ground more fertile. But not The Burn. During The Burn, the people had to deal with the fires. It was in the years after the fires, when fewer and fewer things grew back, when the vestiges of green withered and dried and shriveled into dust, that people realized the horrible truth—humanity had lost the entire steppingstone of agriculture. The very thing that allowed humans to propel themselves up the evolutionary ladder was now lost because of the solar flares.

Numi plucked a plant from the soft earthen womb of the grave, but rather than standing and returning to the trailer right away, she ran her hand over the soft earth. It smelled horrid, and most people of Barning avoided the graveyard, despite its invaluable contents. It was a small pleasure, a privilege worth the gory work, to be able to feel rich soil beneath her hands. The fertile plot of earth was like something from another planet, deposited in a dead landscape. Numi closed her eyes and sunk her hand into the dirt. She didn't worry about damaging the roots of the delicate ground cover—the useful parts were nearly harvested away, and the remaining greens were good for little more than blanching and ingesting as filler to chase away hunger pangs.

As her hand sunk deeper, Numi felt the soft earth change to soppy, heavy sludge. She had reached too far, past the rejuvenated soil, straight down to its source. In this case, the source of the soil's nutrients was a combination of a calf lost to a broken leg last year, several malnourished stray dogs, and, of course, Ursa Rauth. Ursa was too far buried, resting too deep to be the source of the putridness that Numi had sunk her hands into. Still six feet down, Ursa was likely amidst the rubble of a broken coffin. Leaking her remains into the surrounding soil, Ursa gave it new life from her own death and decay.

Numi removed her hand from the earth, clutching a small vertebrate in her fingers. The calf was the rot that now covered her hand. She wiped her hand on her skirts and stood. Ursa was still resting deep beneath the earth, but her corpse could not sustain this plot forever. A few more years perhaps, but then what? Someone would have to take her place. The cycles of nature were inexorably changed, and yet, at their core, remained the same.

Numi's mother, Tamila, had been a teenager when it happened: The Burn. As she grew older, Numi's mother would sometimes reminisce about having just moved out on her own, away from home, when The Burn happened. Not quite old enough to know the things she ought to have, if she had known the world would be ending. Most people of her mother's generation said they didn't think much about those early days—it was the stoic thing to say when The Burn was bought up in conversation.

Numi had never liked that name. The Burn. It felt false, heavy on the tongue like a half-truth swollen with something much larger, much more serious. There were a thousand-and-one names for what had happened, some scientific, some more folklore than truth, but none bothered her quite so much as calling that time The Burn. The Burn felt thick in her mouth, like her body knew it was retching out a lie.

Numi pocketed the goldenrod and made her way to a plot marked only with a foreboding obelisk emblazoned with the name *Strix*. Catnip grew wild along one side of the structure. Numi gathered just as much as she needed and then stood tall. She looked toward her trailer, a dim light in the distance, in the heart of which rested her kitchenette window. It was too far to see Shelly, but if the woman stood, she would block the light bleeding out against the darkness. Shelly was likely sitting quietly, head in her hands. Numi swiftly ducked behind the obelisk, to the north side of the memorial stone, and kneeled, fingers trailing the earth. She grabbed enough of the poisonous nightshade flower for her purposes, stuffing it gingerly into her waist pouch. It was a cruel thing that needed doing, but it needed doing nonetheless.

She stood smoothly and emerged from the other side, as though she had simply strode behind the stone, crossing unceremonious across the lawn, before looping back to her trailer. She wasn't ready to head inside to the cramped, moldy space, but it wouldn't do to leave Shelly alone for too long. There was much to be done tonight.

4.

As she walked back to her trailer, Numi's mind trailed back to her patient. She wondered what she would tell Shelly the next time she came complaining of headaches and nosebleeds.

Numi did what she did in the dark of night—because how could she tell her patient that the corpses in the graveyard were turning to dry bone? Once the corpses finished decomposing, that would be it. Numi had been supplementing the plots with any healthy livestock parts that could be spared, as well as stray animals that she found starved or injured around Barning, but these could only temporarily supplement the existing nutrients in the soil. Like Sisyphus pushing the stone up the hill, with every life she saved, every pig corpse buried, she was simply kicking a can further down the road.

She looked around at the surrounding plots. James, Glasse, Schorn, Moran, Andrews. Each patch of ground once home to a selection of specific plant specimens, ones chosen specifically because they thrived on each individual's unique blend of vitamins, minerals, and nutrients leaching into the soil around them. Most of the plots, once covered in mint, witch hazel, catnip, thistle, and more, were now only a quarter of the size they once were. What was once a gothic Garden of Eden was slowly being reclaimed by the dead earth.

There were grave plots that grew nothing from the outset. Their occupants had been victims of sicknesses that only furthered the barrenness of the soil, poisoning the nearby ground even more. There was also the chance that some of the oldest of the eternal resting places remained miraculously undamaged by the deep fires of those early days, and the occupants slept undisturbed in their coffins. Numi supposed that some people were meant to continue in the endless cycle of life, death, and rebirth, while some were simply removed from the cycle and remained trapped in their own rotting flesh.

So, on this path of circumstances in the decades following The Burn, surviving due to her ingenuity, her blind luck, and her likewise blind foresight, Numi had arrived at this night. One that was reprehensible, unspeakable, but also completely necessary. And even despite her...newly evolved methods...she would, eventually, have to start acting with more discretion. Making choices about who received treatment and who didn't. There were not enough resources left in the world to provide everyone with relief from the things that plagued them. She did not relish the decisions she would need to make when this day came. The longer she could put it off, she would—no matter the cost.

Numi found Shelly still in the kitchenette booth, sitting a little bit taller than she had been ten minutes before. Perhaps it was the tea, or perhaps it was simply the act of sitting quietly with her thoughts. Or maybe it was the expectation of healing.

"How are you feeling?" Numi asked, moving over to the counter and grabbing a small, woven pouch.

"Better," Shelly said. "I think I need some sleep."

"Before you go, let me prepare something to take with you," Numi insisted. It would not help, but Numi believed in the power of the placebo effect as much as she believed in magic and medicine. She placed her pouch on the countertop. She put her back to Shelly, blocking her view of the workspace. No sense causing her any additional anxiety. The poor thing was already in such bad shape.

Numi spread the catnip, goldenrod, and nightshade on the counter and slid her knife from her belt. She cut the catnip down to a reasonable size, followed by the goldenrod, and finally the nightshade. Shelly sat uncomfortably quiet, not making small talk, not nervously chattering like she had before. Some people believed that animals knew when they were dying. They settled in, found a comfortable spot, and simply let it come to them. Perhaps that was Shelly now. Or perhaps she had simply finally accepted that small talk no longer had a place in the world. There was nothing small to talk about.

Numi handed Shelly the small pouch, stuffed with the freshly gathered herbs. "You'll have to wait for them to dry, but these days that doesn't take long. Just heat up some water and pour it over a pinch of that. It should relieve some of the pressure."

"Thank you," Shelly said, standing up. She took the pouch from Numi's hand. Up close, in the brighter light of the kitchenette, the woman looked even worse than she had in the soft light of the nearby booth. Shelly turned to leave, but then stopped, pausing in front of the small set of steps down to the trailer door. She turned back, as though there was something she wanted to say but was unsure how it would be received.

"What is it?" Numi asked.

"What sort of flowers do you think will grow on my grave?" Shelly asked.

This was the first time someone had asked this question. In truth, Numi often didn't know with any amount of certainty what caused certain plants to thrive on soil seeded with the flesh of one human versus another. She had no way of knowing the diets, habits, and genetic makeup of the individuals that had come to rest in the Barning graveyard, but that was not the sort of answer Shelly was after. Sometimes folks came to her for healing, and sometimes they came to her for answers. Shelly was in need of both.

"It is more of an art than a science, a sort of guesswork," Numi said, "but I believe the plant with the highest likelihood of success on your grave would be snowdrops."

5.

A heavy pounding at the door interrupted the moment, and Numi leaned toward the window to see who it was. She was accustomed to unannounced visitors late at night. The knock came again, and Numi yelled in her gravelly voice: "Who is it?"

"It's Ted. I've brought someone to see you."

Numi sighed. It was time, she supposed.

Ted was the father of a young, sickly child. There was little Numi could do for the child with her limited access to real medicine. Besides that, she wouldn't know what to do for him even if she had an entire hospital at her disposal. She wasn't a doctor. She was a glorified apothecary who treated her patients through a combination of folk medicine and spells designed to create a careful placebo effect. But she would not toy with the hearts of parents. Unless Theodore had somehow found a crop of red-tail toad flower and several other waning herbs, there was little she could do to help.

"It's okay. I'm feeling better," Shelly said as she patted Numi's shoulder.

"Shelly," Numi said, desperate to say something truthful to the woman before she left.

Shelly moved to the door and stopped, but she did not look up.

Numi decided then that Shelly wasn't going to die tonight. Or this week. At least not from the symptoms that plagued her now, and not from Numi's hand. "Make sure not to use that all at once. Ration it out slowly," Numi said, inclining her head toward the sachet Shelly now clutched. "Gods only know when I'll be able to get more."

"I understand," Shelly said, opening the door.

"It is not going to get easier," Numi said. "It might not get harder, but things are never going to go back to the way they were many years ago. You must find some way of coming to peace with it so that you can take care of yourself and your family."

"I know," Shelly said. It may have been her imagination, but Numi thought that she saw the woman's shoulders relax just a little. It was amazing how much easier it was for someone to set down the anxiety of existing simply by being given permission to do so. She swung open the door and stepped down, out of the trailer.

"Hey sweet thing," a gruff voice said, directed at Shelly from the darkness beyond the trailer.

"Shut the fuck up, Eddie," Ted grumbled.

Shelly put her head down and took off at a determined pace back in the direction of her home, a bit more stability in her step than when she had arrived. Numi turned to look at the two broad shadows standing below her. This was not quite unexpected, but there was a part of Numi that had wondered if Ted would be the one to back out on their bargain.

"And what do you want?" Numi said, her eyes adjusting to the darkness and fixing on Ted's face.

Before Ted could speak, the other man let out a drunken belch that, somehow, transformed into a sentence. "My buddy here, he says you needs a job doing." He snorted back a laugh, or perhaps another belch, and he straightened himself. "And it just so happens, I'm looking for work. I would even work in exchange for *certain services,* if you're offering." The looming shadow leaned in.

Numi stared at Ted once more. This was not exactly what she had in mind and not what they had discussed. He had clearly lost control over the scenario at some point and had improvised. Greatly. In the dark she saw his rib cage expand as he took a deep breath.

"I told Eddie you could maybe read his fortune," he said. "Come on, Numi, be a good sport. He doesn't believe you're a real witch. He thinks it's just a front for *other* business."

"I'm just passing through," Eddie said. "It's been a long journey, and I'm just a lonely guy. Numi is it? Ted said you needed help with a little problem, and I'm your man. Let your buddy Eddie help out."

"How do you know Ted?" Numi asked, wary of this already. Eddie was big. Strong. He was also drunk. She didn't like what could happen here if things went sideways.

"He's just passing through," Ted echoed. "I gave him some work today. He's an able guy, and I needed some help around our property. He told us about some of his...previous work. And I thought you and he might be able to have a mutually beneficial arrangement."

Numi paused and considered. She may as well see this through. Perhaps Eddie could be of use. "Well, you better hurry up and come in, before you catch a cold," she said, deadpan.

Eddie chortled. "I've seen a lot of things in the past several years. Never met a comedian fortuneteller before, though. This town sure has some weird shit," he said, climbing up into the trailer.

Ted followed him and stood at the far side of the living room. Numi gestured to Eddie, indicating that he should sit in the kitchenette booth. He slid in, pulling a jar of a cloudy, amber liquid from the folds of his clothes. As he unwound the lid of the jar, a sickly-sweet smell met Numi's nostrils, burning slightly.

Numi slid into the booth opposite Eddie and watched him as he took a long swig of the liquid. He maintained eye contact with her, both in distrust and intense interest. Numi had a brief flash of *One Thousand and One Arabian Nights*. An old story from before The Burn, long before. She briefly felt the spirit of the heroine. Numi would need to sell the role of a fortuneteller, lest Eddie decide she was, in fact, actually offering other services. If he decided to help himself, she wasn't sure Ted would be able to do much in the way of defending her.

"Would you like some?" Eddie asked, wiping his mouth and leaning his jar in her direction.

"Actually, I was about to fix myself a cup of tea. Let me make you one and read your leaves. Then you can decide whether I read fortunes, and we can discuss the business at hand."

"And will you ensure that my immediate future is...pleasant?" Eddie asked before barking out another foul-smelling laugh.

6.

"What is your diet like?" Numi asked, examining the whites of Eddie's eyes.

The man laughed and nodded at Ted. "She's fucking with me, right?" he asked, taking a swig from his jar.

"Not yet, I'm not," Numi said. "Now tell me what you've been putting in that gut of yours."

No amount of begging and crying by Ted or his wife could fix the simple problem of resource scarcity. Not unless they found a lucrative method for farming livestock for the sole purpose of slaughter-treating the soil. And that was exactly how they had hatched their dark plan.

"I do just fine for myself," Eddie said with a yellow-toothed smile.

Numi instantly knew his sort. He was one of the ones she thought of as firewalkers. Someone who leaned into this broken world. Eddie no doubt reveled in the opportunities it created for men like him, men with a withered conscience and the strength to take what they want.

Ted's wife did not know about his and Numi's machinations. It was not for Numi to judge Ted's decision on that front. The world had moved on from such concepts as honesty and transparency as an expectation. Hiding the horror in the world from those around you was a way of surviving now. Ted's wife had horrors of her own, things she had witnessed and done to survive, things that only she knew, and there was no need to add more burden to her heart. She did not need to know that Ted hadn't needed help on his property. She did not need to know that Ted didn't bring this man here on a drunken fortunetelling lark. Ted's wife slept in her shelter on this night without the burden of knowledge that Ted and Numi had hatched a murder plan to bring this man before the executioner's axe and use him as fertilizer for her graveyard garden. All so that Numi might grow more red-capped toad flowers in order to treat Ted's son.

"Do you want me to take my shirt off, too?" Eddie asked with a vile wink.

No, Ted didn't intend for this to be the only life sacrificed for that of his son. This was simply the first. To Ted, the life of someone like Eddie was worth a fraction of the life of his son, and, Numi admitted, it was hard to disagree. Eddie was a dangerous sort. He believed in survival of the fittest, and was he so wrong? He was strong and almost healthy. His dark lifestyle had not only allowed him to survive, it helped him to thrive. He was not kept awake at night by the things he had done. He had no circles under his eyes. Though dirty, his skin had the plump and elastic look of someone that drank enough water, which, with the current rations, could only mean he was stealing it from others.

"Maybe later," Numi said. Then she got up swiftly and set about filling her pestle with a particular collection of herbs, quite different from those she had prepared for Shelly.

7.

Numi poured hot water over her concoction of herbs and brought the cup to the table. Eddie reached for it and Numi smacked his hand. He pulled his meaty hand away.

"It must steep," she hissed.

Ed scoffed and took a swig from his jar. He belched and set the nearly empty vessel down loudly. "Load of horseshit if you ask me."

"Humor me," Numi said.

"Whatever you say, sweetheart." He leered, leaning forward. "You know, I bet underneath all that dirt you've got a good body. Rugged. Younger looking than your face."

As the steam rose up in front of Eddie's face, Numi saw it again. The shape in the steam. It was two snakes, weaving in and out, tracing an infinity. One swallowed the other's tale in perpetuity. This time, the symbol pulled a word to her tongue. Yes, an ouroboros. She focused on it, watching as it slid smoothly in the steam, finally dispersing, leaving only an unobstructed view of Eddie's face.

"Or perhaps," Numi said, "I'm hiding a collection of wings and tentacles beneath my skirts."

She showed no sign of humor on her face as she stared at Eddie for a long moment. Once the silence grew uncomfortable, she spoke. "Fine. You seem like a man not easily entertained by tea leaves. Do you want to see real magic? Do you want a glimpse into the heart of darkness?"

His face remained unchanged for a beat, and another again, before he let out a small, confused laugh. "You're a right mad bitch. Yeah, show me your fucking magic tricks, ya twat, and then let's get to what I'm really here for."

Numi stood swiftly and crossed the main living area of the trailer toward the back door.

8.

Truthfully, Numi was simply indulging in a bit of dramatics. She would make a show of reading the man's fortune, and they would both find out their fates.

It may have been grotesque, but Numi did not find it particularly difficult to make a show of reading the entrails of animals and often did so for gullible and well-resourced individuals willing to pay in precious resources and long-lost luxuries in exchange for some particularly theatrical confirmation bias.

What she was actually doing, from a practical perspective when engaging in this grotesque practice, was checking the animal's innards for rot. Tumors, cancers, wasting diseases, anything that could further poison the soil. Such animals were burned, their ashes used for the simplest of employments—inks, charcoals, dyes. The healthy ones, specifically the healthy vultures—free of disease, killed by old age or misadventure—they were useful.

Numi plucked a key from her belt and unlocked the shed behind her trailer. It reeked to high heaven, but Numi had long ago become nose-blind to the saccharine stink. She reached up and hefted the limp corpse of a turkey vulture from a hook. A venerable creature. A royal and sacred creature in Numi's eyes. One to be treated with respect, even, and especially, in death.

For the second time that night, she thought about the fact that no one had ever asked how Numi had managed to grow a fruiting pomegranate tree inside her moldy trailer, but if they had, she might have told them that a turkey vulture's blood is special. They eat the dead and turn them into life-force. If this one appeared free of disease, she would be able to set aside some of the gore to mix in with her beloved fruit tree.

Numi said a silent thank-you to the animal, showing appreciation for the resources it could provide her with, even in death. She exited, locked up the shed, and ascended the stairs back into the trailer. She felt clearer now, more sure. Yes, Eddie was exactly who she needed, actually. He was horrible. Almost a caricature of a Bad Man, and now here he was, sitting at her trailer table, offering to take lives so that she could save others. She understood now that this was exactly who she needed. The answer to the moral quandary that still festered within her.

"What the fuck?" Eddie said when Numi sat the carcass down on the tabletop between them. "Look lady, I don't know what the hell you think I'm here for—"

Numi cut him off. "I know what you think you're here for. You think you're here to fuck me in exchange for killing some folks for me. Is that right?"

Eddie was no longer laughing. He looked uneasy. Animals became dangerous when they were uneasy. "Is that not what I'm here for?"

"Well, let's find out, shall we?" Numi drew her knife from her belt, but this time it was not for breaking down herbs. She drew her knife edge down the breast of the bird. "Let us see what your future holds."

Numi stuck her hand into the bird and dramatically pulled a length of intestine through the opening, stretching it out in the air to full effect. The organ was warm, and its putrid aroma filled the cramped trailer, causing Eddie to belch and cover his face. She laid the entrails down on the table, placing them across the table space in front of her guest. Eddie was morbidly transfixed by the gore laid bare in front of him, but something else caught Numi's attention. She stared into the cavity of the bird, and it was there that she saw it. Amongst the stinking, fetid entrails, hanging out of a hole in the bird's guts, Numi saw a snake.

It had fallen through an incision made in the intestines by Numi's unceremonious, heavy-handed machinations with the blade. A snake, only just barely digested, with its own tail lodged firmly in its mouth. Again, the ouroboros. A symbol of eternity, the infinite cycle of life and death. Yes, yes. Eddie would be perfect.

Numi cleared her throat and sat back, creating distance from herself, the corpse, and Eddie.

"Is it that bad?" Ed asked, forcing a gruff laugh. "Do I have ghosts in my blood?"

"Do not joke about such things," Numi said in a low voice, "lest you invite their attentions." Numi locked eyes with Eddie. "When I look at you, I see death and I see the life that comes from death. Your life is not long, but it is infinite."

Eddie looked at Numi, uncomfortable and uncertain. "Whatever the fuck that means," he said. Looking back at Ted, briefly. Ted looked at Numi and in that moment she saw that he understood. He understood what she had decided and did not move to stop her when next she spoke.

"You can drink your tea now," Numi said to Eddie without looking away from the mess.

Eddie picked up the cup, his killer's hand comically large on the handle, and downed it in a single gulp.

Numi looked up and locked eyes with Ted. "You understand it will not be enough," Numi said.

Ted stared back, a solemn look on his face, and nodded.

"Good," she said.

Eddie's head began to droop.

"Will we need to check him? Make sure he's healthy on the inside?" Ted asked. "Like you did with the bird?"

"Yes, we will have to. But the tea he just drank will keep him from moving." She grabbed the knife and stood, staring at the stinking, muscular sack of limbs draped over her table. "I would prefer not to do this...in here."

9.

Sometime later, they laid Eddie, or whatever his name really was, in a grave at a depth just far enough for the roots of future seedlings to easily reach. She caught sight of the man's chest as it rose and fell shallowly, quickly. She was surprised he was still alive, even if only just barely.

She thought she would feel something. Perhaps justifications bubbling to her lips, a defensive display supporting the insanity of her choice. But the world was insane now, wasn't it? He had said it himself. He was simply traveling through. He would not be missed.

Numi shoveled the dirt into the cavity and basked in the nothingness she felt as the man began to disappear beneath the earth. She envisioned the Barning graveyard as it could be—a biome of once-endangered and threatened species and perhaps new, never-before seen ones as well. Yes, she could see it now, the patch of foxglove three times its current size. The Scottish thistle nearly self-sustaining. Enough hen of the woods to sustain many of the inhabitants of Barning. Perhaps enough that they would begin to see a great many children again and keep those children alive.

Numi didn't feel the need to look back, either to the past or to the grave in which they had just buried Eddie. There was much to do. She would need to take inventory of her henbane and her valerian root. There would need to be a conversation with Ted to plan ahead.

As they walked back to the trailer, they did not say a word. Numi would need to clean up the mess she had made in her kitchen with the turkey vulture, but the thought wasn't an unpleasant one. She was seeing the world anew, through a lens of new possibility. Perhaps the circle of life was not broken, but simply changed for the stranger.

Who Dies?

Chloe Viner

There are people who
wish to live but die
and those who
wish to die but live
like a breeding dog caged claws
growing into paw pads
depression digs in
an insult
to loved lives lost

Do they watch now?
curse my inability to make
cloth from yarn?
bread from flour?
happiness from
happy moments?

Can I live in the middle
the battle where opposing sides
stop to share a cigarette?

No,
I'll either hike away from
every moment that
broke me
or die alone
in the woods

For Eva

Paul Carro

The last thing to die at the end of the world is someone's past. One would think an apocalypse would signal a restart, but one would be wrong. Survivors will forever be known by their former actions. A shame, really, given that many people did certain things to get by. Does that make them all bad people? Probably. Am I one of them? Probably. As I stood in a field and watched a wagon approach, I realized I could not even pick apples without my past catching up to me.

I lived on the outskirts of a little town called Barning that did its best to survive day to day. Good people there—most of them—if one did not dig into their past lives. The town comprised people of all types with one thing in common: they were survivors. Certain groups made alliances, and many tried to drag me into their tribes, but I'm not a joiner. My little piece of land remained far outside of town, leaving me beyond their protection, but I didn't need it. I could take care of myself.

Except I had gotten sloppy, complacent, or maybe I just wanted to pick apples in peace and not think of one more danger, one more problem rearing its ugly head in the closest place to an oasis that I knew to exist. An unexpected visitor should not have surprised me, since the first thing that dies at the end of the world is peace.

Word of my past traveled as much as I had. Those looking to make a name would occasionally seek me out to test me. I assumed the driver of the approaching wagon was one such individual. Pointless to run. I was too far from my home and my weapons. The stranger's horses looked well fed; good for them, because the man in the driver's seat appeared on the verge of starvation. The wagon was old-school, chuck-wagon style with a canvas arch covering the bed. Sitting high on the wooden driver's seat, the man held the reins in one hand. In his other, he held a shotgun, which he kept pointed at me.

"Hello neighbor," I said, despite never seeing him before. I took a bite of one of my apples from the bunch I had collected in a basket at my feet. It was tasty.

"I'm looking for Angus West," the spindly man said.

The man came from the Outer. Different people had different names for it, but the Outer was areas long ago abandoned, the elements too harsh, the resources too limited to offer chances of life. Danged if some people did not make a go of it, though. Maybe my wagon-riding friend was one.

His clothes were the tell. A once-upon-a-time white onesie was his uniform of choice. Spots of white showed through, the fabric's original color before the elements got to the garb, which was now mostly brown, green, and black, the colors of dirt and misery. The stranger also wore a scarf around his face and goggles that made his eyes look googly. The goggles were not a type that would protect against the sun, but they would keep other elements at bay, especially when traveling through a dust bowl.

I might have been curious and inquired about his journey, but not while he pointed a shotgun at me. There was likely no one else in the vehicle. No way to know for certain, but safe to assume any passengers would have poked their heads out at the sudden stop.

So there I was, me and a stranger, him with a gun aimed at me. Like I said, I can take care of myself. The man never saw it coming when I hurled the apple. The half-bitten missile struck him in the temple. He made a strange squeal when the apple hit with a loud crack. The stranger tipped over the edge of the wagon and acquainted himself with the ground.

The fall stunned him, but he was stunned further when I relieved him of his weapon and pointed it at his right eye, pressing the barrel against his goggle lens. The man's other eye went extra googly, and he raised his arms. We studied one another for a time before he finally found his voice.

"It's not loaded."

I pulled the trigger to test his theory. It clicked, and he screamed despite himself. I left the man prone on the ground while I introduced myself to the horses. The man stood, highly offended.

"How did you know I wasn't lying about it not being loaded?" he asked.

"I didn't. Lucky for you, it was the truth. Foolish to come after me without an actual weapon," I said.

Guns were scarce, but bullets were more so in the modern world. The horses appeared healthy. I gave each an apple, and they eyed me with delight. I think I made a couple of friends. They whinnied with satisfaction as I gave each a hardy pat down. Takes a lot to feel anything when you're so big. Sun might have shit the bed on the world, but creatures kept on breathing. End of the world was good for many an animal. Got back to nature, most of them. I glanced in the wagon's rear before returning my attention to the horses.

"Two minutes. Talk," I said.

"I'm looking for Eva."

"Eva doesn't exist," I said.

I disliked folklore. Many people lost their lives looking for clean waterways or safe havens that did not exist. Folklore meant hope. Hope should have died when the sun burped, but it did not. Hope reared its head occasionally, just often enough to get people in trouble. The folklore about Eva told of a woman building a polite society somewhere in the big city. Beautiful, smart, resourceful, dangerous. My kind of woman. Too bad she was nothing but bullshit.

"She exists." He pulled a map from his outfit and opened it against the canvas backing of the wagon.

A big red circle and the name Eva were the highlight of a map of downtown Montpelier. I rolled my eyes. They had clearly taken the man for his valuables. Duped.

"How much did you pay for this map?" I asked.

"You saw my wagon was empty, right?"

Everything. The man gave everything for a map. For Eva. Eva of the stories. Eva who did not exist. He had no barter sense, but he had enough wits to notice how I subtly checked the wagon interior. I offered an inventory.

"Hay for the horses, a briefcase, and an Igloo cooler. I have not seen a cooler like that in a long time. What's in it?"

"My wife," he said.

After introductions, I was soon on the road with the man. Norm was his name. Candace was his wife, and she rode in the back inside the Igloo cooler. Her bones, at least. As for the briefcase? That was why I chose to accompany the man on his foolish quest. I very much wanted what was in the briefcase.

The contents were my payment if I delivered him to Eva. To be clear, I made a deal to deliver Norm to the red circle on the map, not to Eva, since I was certain she did not exist. Norm reluctantly agreed to the terms while hoping to prove me wrong. I knew I was correct, so arranged for payment even if the journey's outcome did not go as planned. Traveling to Montpelier under a sun which had long ago turned against humans was a fool's mission. We waited until sundown. After loading water, jerky, and the apples, we set out on the road.

The wagon had lantern poles on both sides of the seating, which, along with the moon, lit our way. It would take about eight hours to arrive. That would allow us time for a pit stop along the way. Wagon travel is tiresome. We planned to stick mostly to the major thoroughfares, despite the enormous number of abandoned vehicles and forest over-growth along the way. Nature had reclaimed much of what man had once made, but the same roadways remained relatively flat and work-able for the horses.

We were two hours in when the man got gabby. They always get gabby.

"My wife wished so desperately to meet Eva. Eva lives by the stan-dards my wife strived for. Candace was resourceful but loathe to engage in subterfuge. My wife was an honest woman. They say the same about Eva. Eva looks people in the eyes when she speaks to them. How many people can say that?"

"Half the people in the world have sun-damaged eyes. Can't blame folks if they cannot meet a person's gaze."

"Eva hugs people, so happy to meet them. She welcomes the hud-dled masses, the tired, the poor. She looks out for them, not herself," he said wistfully, holding the reins.

The horses had a pep in their step from the apples. We trotted along fine, though Norm appeared intent on having a new thought for every clop of the horses' hooves.

"How did your wife die?" I asked.

"The sun disease. Nothing but a bird by the end, a little angel bird."

Weren't many birds in the world anymore. The sky choked them all out. I saw one occasionally, but rumors they used to sing were another folktale, as fake as Eva, I assumed. I nodded when he stated her cause of death. Too many people lost to the same thing supposed to keep us alive. The world was for shit. At least there were horses.

"We were looking for Eva. Travelled to several horrible places in search of her. But Candace got the sun disease and gave up on breathing before I secured the map. I burned my wife. Hurt to do so, but I knew of no other way to deliver her to where she wished to go. If Eva takes me in, I will gladly call it my new home. But even if Eva does not, I can deliver Candace to her. They say Eva buries the dead with ceremony and respect. Eva believes in traditions and old ways."

"Whoever 'they' is, they sure talk a lot," I said.

"I understand. You don't believe, but Eva proves people wrong. She treats the worst among us as worthy of kindness."

"And I am the worst among us?" I asked, not offended at all. Simply curious.

"You kill. Efficiently. That was what I was told. That was why I sought you out. I knew what payment might entice you."

The briefcase. He was correct. I barely listened while he told me where he found it. I looked at the horses.

"Your horses are well cared for," I said.

"The least among us. Grass and hay are two things not in short supply, at least in some abandoned parts of the world. It doesn't take much beyond effort. Besides, they were my wife's favorites. Many a time, we feared marauders might take the horses from us. Will there be marauders where we are heading?"

Marauders were bad news. They existed in all places where people breathed, but like most cowards, they kept hidden until assembled in a gang. They killed for fun; no reasoning with them. While marauders would collect goods from their victims, they acted for the thrill, not for supplies. Most were well armed, or as well as anyone could be in such times.

"Yes, Norm. There will be marauders."

"Do you think they will try to kill us?"

"With great enthusiasm. Not too late to back out."

"No. Candace needs to be put to rest."

"Montpelier it is then. Let's allow the horses and ourselves a rest. We will still arrive by morning."

Despite Norm having traveled from the Outer, the sight of a dead city caused the man to gasp in awe. The horses reacted as well, not to the sights but to the smells. Food from generations past had gone to spoil, and decomposing bodies were plentiful. Most of the rot had faded, but the fungus growing in the same spots where people fell brought with it a lingering sweet scent of decay.

Norm proved a decent driver, especially considering how often we needed to go off the road because of the wreckage from long past. I used the time to memorize the map. I had traveled to many places in my past, back when I needed to provide for someone important to me. She was no longer around, so I had ceased traveling across what remained of the world and had settled into the role of apple-picker. I had a good sense of where exactly we were going by the time we arrived.

A dead city towered above us. The crumbling manmade obelisks would soon provide cover from the sun or amplify it, depending on where we stood. The rays of the sun would force us to consider every step, and movement itself would become tactical. I dressed much like my traveling companion but wore pants and a jersey hoodie rather than a one piece. I needed more mobility than my new friend.

The jersey read Hampshire College. The name meant nothing to me, though I realized at one point how we were a world of time-travelers now, living in places built by generations past, wearing the clothes of people long gone. People of another time would attach memories to the simplest of items, but in the present, they meant nothing other than another day of survival. Norm mentioned how he found the briefcase in a similar place. The briefcase that would become my payment.

It was shocking that the briefcase's contents remained untouched. Perhaps the cabin he found it in was difficult to get to, in the sun's direct path for most of the day. There were places that were mostly untouchable because of their positioning on the poisoned earth. Some parts of the world were much worse than others, not worth the effort to explore and chance finding nothing more than an untouched can of beans. Norm got lucky with the briefcase.

When the sun decided it was time for a planet cleansing, it did so in fits and starts. Places like Barning somehow maintained some sort of cosmic cover, which was why people settled there. Ozone, I heard someone call it once. But many other places became testaments to the power of the glowing orb in the sky. Blisters were one sign of the sun disease, while others died quickly from exposure.

In the big cities, bones lay scattered about. We already passed plenty while riding down a city street, rolling into a world of high rises. The sun had baked many of the corpses, mummifying flesh into a flaky texture. When the winds whipped in certain directions, it scattered the dried flesh, which was why we wore handkerchiefs and goggles.

I doused the wagon lanterns as the sky mixed into a blend of gray and orange. Sunrises were a threat, and a new one had just begun. We were further east than Barning, so the sun rose a bit earlier than I planned. The sun brought with it dangers of various types. The horses whinnied. I knew I liked them. They sensed the danger. A sign on a tall structure to our left read "parking."

"In there," I said.

"That's not the place on the map," Norm said.

I liked his answer. It meant he had memorized the map as well. He knew where we were going. I nodded in agreement.

"It's for the horses. We need to go on foot."

We pulled into a large open space, free of vehicles and dead people. I leaped off and helped Norm maneuver the wagon so that the horses faced the wide exit. Then I loosely placed the reins against a nearby pipe running the length of a cement wall, likely a water or sewage line back when such things existed.

"That's not tied down," Norm complained.

"I want them to make it out if we do not. It should fool them enough to remain for now, but if we never return, they will be free to leave when they figure things out."

I fed the beasts two apples each, then spread hay on the concrete at their feet. I pulled out the bowl I brought along with my supplies and poured water into it. The horses would keep long enough.

"Won't the marauders steal everything?" Norm asked.

"Not before they attempt to kill us. The horses are safe for now. We will know when the marauders discover our presence. We will have an early warning system in place."

Norm and I took time to eat, to get our strength up. I hid the briefcase in a space underneath the wagon.

"Won't we need that?" Norm asked.

"These people will kill for what's in that briefcase, and its presence would remove any stealth."

I checked my blades. Everything in its place. I handed a knife to Norm, who shook his head.

"Eva does not believe in killing," Norm said.

"Then you've proven she doesn't exist."

"How so?"

"No one lives in a city without killing," I said, matter of fact.

"Not Eva. Never Eva. Mercy has she on those who wish her harm. She forgives them."

"After they kill her? Quite a feat."

"Before. She captures them, rehabilitates them," Norm said with conviction. "Therefore, I do not kill."

I handed him the shotgun.

"Won't they also kill for this?"

"Yes, if they dare get close enough. Besides, you're not above clubbing someone unconscious, are you? Does Eva frown on that?"

"I suppose if my life was in danger," Norm said.

"Trust me, it is."

We patted the horses and set out on foot. The sun was rising quick. The buildings achieved what I hoped they would by supplying shadow zones. We moved in the shade. I urged Norm to remain close to the buildings. We traveled about a mile on foot, nothing too daunting except that some buildings were not high-rises—smaller stores, bodegas, and apartments from a time gone by.

Those smaller buildings cast smaller shadows and left us exposed. As we passed one such place, Big Eddy's sandwich shop, I heard it. Glass shattered somewhere high above and nearby.

"Move!" I yelled.

Norm did but was uncertain about the sudden urgency. Another window shattered a block away. That was their early warning signal. Smash the glass in their lookout windows. No sense looking for those in the lofty towers. They would only survive on shade-facing sides of a building. It would be difficult to spot them. They were not the threat, anyway; they were too far away. The real threat made itself known as the sound of horse hooves clomping. They had their own animals, ones not tethered to a wagon, which meant maneuverability.

They appeared in the near distance. Four on horseback. The first barreled toward us, the rider waving a machete. I grabbed Norm and turned down an alley. Mistake. Several marauders stood at the other end. More machetes.

The group at the mouth of the alley was not on horseback. They wore thick clothing, as if the heat of the sun did not bother them. Their uncovered faces revealed an impressive collection of boils.

We had no choice now. One horse at our rear and more on the way. We had to go through. I heard the group ahead laugh when I pulled out a knife. Who brings a knife to a machete fight? But I used the distance to my advantage and threw the blade, which caught the first in the throat. The man grabbed at the wound and gargled through flowing blood before dropping to his knees. He reached out, trying to grab something, likely his escaping life. He did not catch it. The man fell face-first, driving the blade deeper.

The fallen body slowed the two men behind him. But behind us, the original horseback rider came on fast, riding through the luminous space with no problem. His machete scraped against one wall when he raised it to strike. He did not need the blade to take Norm and me down, since the horse could do the work for him. There was no time. The horse was at full speed, happy to work out its legs.

Norm and I positioned ourselves so that we faced the oncoming horse directly. Norm pointed the shotgun as a threat, and it worked. The rider lifted his machete arm across his face to block a potential shot. That was all the time I needed. I shoved Norm against the wall and pushed myself flat against the other as the horse rode past, barely missing us both. I slapped the horse's rear as hard as possible.

The horse sped up, causing the rider to drop his blade as he wrestled for control of the frightened beast. Then the two other men in the alley's mouth screamed as the horse leapt over the dead body and struck them in flight. The men tumbled to the ground. Not a direct hit, no cracking of skulls. The fallen men would rise.

I was already in motion, picking up the rider's machete and slicing the throats of both marauders before they could find their footing. The horse continued running. It would take some time for the man to calm it down. We only needed seconds and were now out of view of the eyes in the sky. The other three horses from earlier drew closer, their clopping sounding down the alley. It would not be long before they followed. However, the fallen bodies would slow them down significantly.

We emerged from the alley and hugged a wall. In a city like this, where the marauders were half-cooked, there would only be so many of them. In smaller cities, marauders were normal citizens who gathered to kill, maim, torture, and steal. Here, they were a community, but the sun would have taken many in their prime. There could only be so many eyes in the skies. If we followed the walls of the buildings, those straight above us would have no view.

We still chanced being seen by others in high-rises somewhere, but it would take massive numbers to occupy anything more than a mile at a time. At the least, no more early warning glass sounded as we moved block after block. The horses never emerged from the alley, which bought us more time. They likely detoured back the way they came. But they would be on us soon enough. As it was, I heard the single clop of hooves as the original rider regained control of his horse.

They had proved themselves well organized, acting as a family, survivors living in the mouth of hell. I had no illusions they wanted anything from us other than blood. There would be no reasoning with them. Nothing we could say would quell their bloodlust. Madness took hold of many a person who suffered the lingering effects of the brutal sun. In most cases, the individual soon expired from exposure. If these men made it through long enough to survive, they were likely mad. These were not normal marauders.

It was not a kill-*or*-be-killed situation but a kill-*and*-be-killed one. Nothing would stop them. Nothing. I guessed their numbers to be small based on survivability, but if I was wrong, their numbers would win out in the end. I promised Norm that I would deliver him to Eva, and I intended to keep that promise. If we were to have it out with the locals, it would have to be there.

We were close. Our destination was a former hotel, the building standing higher than those surrounding it. We saw it from a distance as we first approached. Someone had drawn a crude image of the building on the map, the one which Norm traded everything for.

Norm quickly tired as we ran. The food we had consumed was not enough to fuel the man. He struggled with the gun and the cooler. I stopped him, took the gun, and tossed it aside. He looked relieved. But, as was his way, he protested to the end.

"Why did you do that?" Norm asked.

"It is no longer a benefit but is slowing us down. You point it at them again, and they'll remove it from your grip by slicing off your hands. Now, your wife, Candace, you hold onto her with everything you've got. She's all that is important right now. Nothing else. Not you, nor I. You got it?"

He nodded. We were dead—check. But get Candace there? Can do. We occasionally lost sight of the building as we ran, too close to other structures to see beyond them, but we were making good time. Too good. I knew something Norm did not.

Norm was not the only damn fool to buy a map. Others would do the same in the quest for a world of peace, a world that could change for the better, run by a woman named Eva. They knew. The reason the marauders were not on our tail was because they waited for us at the hotel. They understood the idea of hope would lead people to their doom.

The question was, could I hold off the horde long enough to allow Norm to deliver his wife? Unlikely. Soon, we were there. It was silent. Too silent. We approached from an alley, stepped out into the street, and I looked both ways. They were there, as expected. Waiting on horseback on either end of the street. Two horses on either end, three men each behind them on foot. They would converge any second.

Sliding glass doors loomed ahead, an entrance to the magical building that held the answers to saving the world. Taking in our situation, I wished someone like Eva existed. The glass was murky but intact, an oddity in a fallen city. The doors were closed. Whether they were operable remained a question, but we had to get to them first. So close, but not close enough.

I raised the machete and looked from one end of the street to the other. I nodded toward the entrance and yelled to Norm.

"Go! Run, Norm!"

The man at the other end of the street smiled. I understood our mistake immediately. They were not charging us for a reason. I shoved Norm and told him to get to the door, and then I took off, running toward the closest group. Two arrows *thwipped* past, striking where we were just standing. Archers. That was why the men had not advanced on us yet.

They staged archers high above the hotel known to draw foolhardy folks, those longing for a better life—Eva's way. Shooting from a high-rise across the street, they would snuff pilgrims out one by one. By running toward one of the flanking groups, I removed myself as a target. Shoot at me, shoot at them. But Norm was in the wind. I hoped he could get inside.

With the game changed, the two men on horseback charged, followed close behind by the three men on foot. The first rider passed with a swing of his blade. I ducked, rolled, and rose in time to face off against the second horseman. I sliced and removed the man's leg. The amputated limb changed the rider's center of gravity, and he slid off the horse, screaming in pain.

Three marauders on foot surrounded me. Though armed, the men were not skilled. I could tell they were hungry. Probably skin and bones underneath their garb. That was why they dressed the way they did in the deadly heat. They hoped to be imposing.

Two of the marauders swung at once. I blocked simultaneously with my machete and kicked the legs out from the one closest to me. He went down on his face. Blood spurted from somewhere around his jaw, likely where he bit his own tongue off or lost some teeth. He was no longer a threat. He remained on the ground, crying over spilled blood.

I heard a thump and a cry. The group at the other end of the street remained in place, though their horses danced, eager to join the battle. An arrow flew at Norm. The force propelled him into the glass doors. Thankfully, Candace took the arrow for him. The projectile stuck out of the Igloo cooler. The shot knocked him for a loop, however. He was a sitting duck. I needed to get him to cover.

The remaining two marauders pressed the attack, while the one on horseback trotted alongside, looking for an opening. I sliced one of the attacker's arms, the one holding his blade. His arm went limp and lifeless. He was out of the fight. I elbowed him in the face for good measure, which dropped him on his ass. He was happy to remain there.

The last one was the most skilled, but the horseman moved in now that it was a one-on-one fight. The horse-rider swung his blade. I surprised the last foot soldier by dropping my blades. Rushing the marauder, I grabbed his loose clothing and spun the man, using him as a shield to take the blade of the man on the horse. I then grabbed the dead man's hand and used its machete to impale the stomach of the rider

The horse-rider slumped in his seat as his life took the fastest route out of him. His horse trotted away slowly, unconcerned with the machinations of man. The rider, to his credit, held the seat for half a block before tumbling onto the street.

Now I was in the open for the archers. I ran, yelling to Norm, who struggled with the glass in the distance. The group at the end of the street advanced then held, waiting for the archers to do their work.

"Open it! Open it now!"

"I'm trying!"

Norm had been lucky. There was now half a quiver of arrows jutting from his cooler and the ground where they failed to penetrate the glass doors. Arrows *thwipped* in my direction as I ran. The speed at which they fired suggested two archers. A life sentence for those high in buildings. The sun would get them eventually, but not before they got us. Their focus on me temporarily took their attention away from Norm.

Possibly frustrated at missing me, they refocused on the easy target. They had immediate success. Norm cried out as an arrow shot through his leg. The projectile jutted out from both sides of his leg. He kneeled, screaming in pain.

I was close enough to notice Norm had opened the doors by a few inches. I reached him just as an arrow took his shoulder. He did not scream, merely cried out with a heavy breath and slid to the ground. The third one took him through the back into his chest, a spot where all the necessary parts would be. Not good. He went down, wheezing.

That was enough for the foot soldiers at the end of the street. They began their advance. I was growing tired; it would be tougher to take them down. My immediate concern was Norm. He groaned but in a raspy way, struggling to breathe.

I placed my hands into the gap of the sliding glass doors and, with great effort, pried them open enough to step inside. I grabbed Norm, pulled him, laying him on his side. Then I pushed the metal frames of the doors closed again.

They designed the doors for electricity. Absent that, they were difficult to slide open or closed. The glass was heavy, tempered, and the doors were oversized. Closing them would slow the pursuers down. Briefly. We were in a grand lobby, one surprisingly clean, considering how long ago the cities became inhabitable.

I turned Norm over. If I put pressure on his wounds, I could delay the inevitable, but I couldn't say that was the merciful thing to do. The group from down the street made their appearance outside the glass, but then they stopped. It made no sense. They simply growled in frustration at the glass.

None tried to enter. They just stood outside. Before long, they appeared to remember their own fallen and went about attending to their wounded and dead. But they no longer pursued us. It made little sense, but I would have to figure it out later. Norm screamed in pain.

He grabbed one of the protruding arrows to pull it out. Big mistake. He screamed in agony and kicked the ground. While I was relieved the group remained at bay, I still moved Norm further away from the door. I dragged him along to the furthest space in the lobby that remained partially lit by outside ambient light. It was an elevator bank out of view of the windows.

Once upon a time, the hotel would have been the height of luxury. Now it was a fancy morgue. The opulence of the place was hard to miss. A crystal chandelier loomed over the largest section of the lobby. The sun's reflection through the crystals would be an eventual death sentence in today's blazing world. I was surprised that no one had torn it down over the years. Why had the place remained relatively untouched while the rest of the city had been ransacked? Why had the group of marauders stopped pursuing us?

Could it be Eva? Did the idea of such a woman extend to those outside? Had superstition raised its head? There was no other reason the marauders did not break into the hotel. Even if the idea of such a woman as Eva stopped them, I figured man's base instincts would soon kick in. There was a group outside who desired revenge for the damage I had done.

I had to assume I was running out of time in a different manner than Norm. I propped him up against a wall, where we remained partially hidden in shadow. Positioning him so the wall did not put pressure on the projectiles was difficult. There was no longer such a thing as comfort for the man.

"Did we make it?" he wheezed.

"Yes, Norm. Yes, we did."

"And Eva? Is she here?"

I didn't want to lie to the man, but I realized I did not have to. There was something to the troops staying outside.

"The idea of her? Yes. The thought of Eva being here was enough to keep marauders at bay."

"No. She is real. She is not simply an idea. I know it. My wife knew it," he said, then coughed into a jag that seemed endless. He reached up and grabbed my hand. He was cold. "Either way, we made it. Thank you."

Norm's eyes settled on mine until they faded. His hand slipped and landed on the cooler that now rested at his side. In the end, the man died with his wife in his arms.

I looked up and would have laughed if I had not just lost the man in my charge. The job was complete, more fully than I first realized. I delivered Norm exactly where he wished to go. For there, spelled out on the wall above where he sat in a pool of his own blood, were letters on the wall.

The letters were large, raised black blocks. Easy to read. Once upon a time, the letters had read *elevator*. But now, with time's passage, the letters on either end had fallen away, leaving only the middle three. The remaining letters above the elevator doors spelled out a name.

Eva.

There above the elevators was a word filled with hope in a hopeless world. Three letters spelled out the name of a woman who did not exist, but the thought of her could make people wish to be better. I was uncertain if I was one, for though Norm longed to have a burial for his wife with ceremony, I could not accommodate such a thing. My job was done.

In the end, he was with his wife. I did what I could, and my mission was complete. Norm and Candace would forever live in the presence of *Eva*. I left while the marauders were still busy tending to their own.

I searched for a fire exit and slipped into a back alley. Without a traveling companion, I could move more stealthily and got back to the carriage without incident. The horses were happy to see me. I named them Candace and Norm and vowed to take good care of them.

I retrieved the briefcase and opened it. Inside was a perfectly preserved revolver and a string of bullets. A firearm from yore in perfect condition. A weapon of war designed for men like me. My payment was complete.

Norm had asked whether it would have helped us. No, the noise would have merely brought the enemy in greater numbers. This was mine to keep for my future. I thought of the idea of Eva and how the thought of such a person was enough to keep even marauders at bay. Maybe the world could eventually live in peace, but until such a time, I had my gun. In honor of Eva, I hoped I would never have to fire it. I got the wagon moving, happy to head home and pick apples and just get by.

The elevator doors slid open, revealing a platform attached to a pulley system. The platform rose from below the hotel and stopped just shy of the lobby floor by about a foot. A man in charge of the rope yanked harder to bring it level. Three more individuals stood inside the elevator beside the pulley operator. Two men, dressed in tactical gear and armed with rifles, emerged.

The two men moved through the lobby with practiced precision. Noticing the chaos outside, they exchanged confused looks about the state of the marauders. They made their way back toward the still-open elevator and shouted simultaneously.

"Clear!"

A woman with long, flowing hair and a kind face stepped from the elevator. She, too, wore tactical gear. She quickly noticed the slumped man in the lobby. The guards moved in instinctively as she leaned down to the visitor on the floor, but the woman motioned the men away. Pulling out a large knife, she cut the strap of the container away.

Opening the cooler, she nodded in recognition. The woman called over her shoulder. "Get reinforcements. We have two. They did not make it. We will give them a proper burial. Side-by-side. Alert the marauders that we demand safe passage. I'll stay with the couple until you return. I imagine they traveled a long way, and it's the least I can do."

The guards stepped into the elevator, and they descended, off to take care of issues from a world hidden beneath their feet. Once the men were gone, the woman started a conversation with the fallen couple.

"Hello. You don't know me, but you are welcome here. And you will be okay. We will take care of you. My name is Eva."

The Double Cross

Joseph Carro

I had the sons of bitches in my crosshairs, and they didn't even know it. The three of them stood in a semi-circle, waving their ridiculous guns around in the air like useless cocks. *Old*, useless cocks, really, if I was going to be the one to use that particular analogy. They looked to be hunting rifles from back before The Collapse. My own gun, Betsy, was no spring chicken herself. Bought her from some old codger up in Maine who told me she was a "Baker Cavalry shotgun," but she'd had some enhancements over time. Next to peashooters, Betsy was a wiry teenager with fire in her veins.

"Adelaid *Hackett!*" one of the men screamed, emphasizing my last name. He had a droopy eyelid on the left side of his face that made me sick if I looked at it too long. His name was Reggie Durham.

"Get your whore ass out here and deal with the consequences of your *actions!*" he yelled.

Whore ass. I reminded myself to shoot him somewhere he was going to feel it before I let him die.

"The longer you make us look for you, the more we're gonna make you suffer. Be smart, you dumb bitch."

I gritted my teeth, took my itchy finger away from the trigger, although it pained me not to shoot the cocksucker between the eyes. *All in good time.* The three of them had "chased" me here to this outcropping of granite cliffs next to some young trees and scrub—just as I'd planned—and I wasn't about to let my anger fuck that up. They were full of piss and vinegar on account of me having stolen right from under their noses for so long, taking money and supplies from each of them until they finally figured out it was me who'd done it, though they'd done a lot of finger-pointing at each other beforehand. A little skimming off the top, that was my specialty. But these were no fuckin' angels. Some of the things they did...well, let's just say I wouldn't have put past myself doing them for survival, so I guess I'm no angel either. But some of the *other* things? Downright sadistic and depraved. They did things that chilled my blood, and that's no small measure. No, these three cocksuckers *deserved* to die, and deserved all the ills to befall them *before* and all the hellish nightmares that waited for them in Hades *after* I was done here today.

Reggie was licking his lips, aiming with his one good eye down the iron sights of the rifle, trying to find some sign of me, some wisp of hair, some disturbance in the dust. There was a squeak to my right, which surprised me a little due to my current stresses, and Reggie swung his gun barrel toward the sound and fired. Black powder filled the air, and something scrambled out from under the granite rocks. I stayed as still as I could, not moving but an inch. The bullet knocked off a sizable chunk of rock from the outcropping, and the air grew still and tense.

"What the *fuck* was that?" Reggie said, waving the smoke away. He began immediately reloading his rifle. He couldn't do it as fast as I could. *Good.*

"Rabbit," said the tallest one in the group, Boston Steve. "I don't think Addie squeaks like that, Reg." They called him Boston Steve because that's where his family was *from*, nothing more to it. Never heard anything in my life so fuckin' anti-climactic as that.

Reggie grimaced and looked like he was going to haul off and punch Steve in the face.

"Stop your yapping and fan the fuck out," Reggie said.

I carefully picked up a rock with my right hand and threw it over to the left, toward the trees. The rock clattered against some other stones and caused the three men to swing their attention to that direction.

"Must've scared her with that shot, Reg," said the shortest one of the group, Renoir. "Bet she's clambering away just like that rabbit." They called him Renoir because he made "art," which primarily consisted of drawings of tits and asses on women that didn't look real. At least not like any of the women I'd ever seen, including my *fuckin' self*. He was named after some famous artist from another country, but his own art didn't look anything like that old stuff—it looked like shit. I once found an old book with pictures of them paintings inside of it. Before The Collapse, it seemed like everyone wanted to paint tits.

"Well, go *get* her then," Reggie said. "Fuck."

I moved as low to the ground as I could, to my right. I had to be quick; I had to be quiet. A couple of times my boots almost rolled as I stepped on loose rocks, but I caught myself and didn't make noise enough for the cocksuckers to catch. I just kept moving forward, inch by inch, keeping the granite shield on my left. The sun was out, and I could smell the heat coming off the stone. Soon it'd be too hot to be out in the sun. When I closed my eyes, I could see lights swimming around inside my lids. Wasn't usually a good sign. It meant the sun was about to get ornery within the next few days.

Reggie nodded and waved his arm in the direction I threw the rock. Steve pulled out his hunting knife and stalked over to where they thought I might be, ready to stick me with it. The blade gleamed in the sun's light. Renoir covered Steve while Reggie scanned the area.

I moved myself into position, a spot I'd chosen the day before, when I knew they'd be coming after me. I rested my gun barrel on a piece of granite for stability and took aim at the back of Renoir's head. I'd already played out this scenario in my own head a hundred times since last night. Just a few more moments, a few more steps, and Boston Steve was going to kick off the fuckin' festivities.

"I don't see any sign of her over here, Reg," said Renoir, lifting his hat from his head to wipe the sweat from his brow. "She's crafty. She must've snuck away by now. Damn shame, too. Was looking forward to gettin' my dick wet."

Oh, your dick wet? I can sure oblige you with that, you fuckin' cock-sucker. I frowned and moved my sights away from his head and then took aim at his crotch. The head would be too fast for the likes of that titty-drawing son of a bitch.

Then, just as I'd planned, Boston Steve stepped in the rusty bear trap. It was hidden among the smaller stones, and it snapped shut with a sickening noise of metal blades hitting flesh and sinking into bone. Steve clutched his leg and screamed and hollered like a madman. I fired off a shot with Betsy, my shotgun, and sprayed Renoir's pecker and up-per thighs with shot, which bowled him over and sprayed blood all over the rocks.

"There's your wet pecker, motherfucker!" I couldn't help but shout as I clambered to a standing position.

Reggie started running, just like I knew he would. I had already started running myself, unsheathing my Bowie knife and pumping my legs as fast as I could after him. He veered right and headed for the cave. Thank the Lord above for predictable bastards.

Dumb son of a bitch.

Reggie disappeared into the cave, swallowed up by the shadows. I stopped just short of the entrance, and a shot rang out as I tried to poke my head around the corner. I moved back away from the cave mouth quickly as one of Reggie's bullets struck a rock somewhere behind me. I heard Boston Steve screaming from back where his leg was all mangled, and Renoir's balls were dripping blood.

"You bitch! You fucking bitch!" Reggie screamed from within the cave. Another shot rang out, then another. He was scared, and he was furious at having been bested by me.

"Reggie," I shouted into the cave. My voice echoed against the rocks. "You're going to die here today, cocksucker. There's no ifs or buts about it."

I ducked back, thinking he was going to fire on me on account of me making him so scared and angry. Sure enough, he did. A piece of rock blasted out from the cave entrance where the bullet struck. That time, I'd let my eyes adjust to the cave darkness while I was talking, and I'd seen him load his gun and then aim before I ducked back. I grabbed another rock and then threw it in his direction. He saw it coming, as I knew his paranoid self would, and he ducked. That gave me time to point my gun at where he'd be seconds before he popped back up, and I pulled the trigger and let his face have the payload. His spasming finger fired off another shot reflexively, which hit somewhere on the ceiling before he fell, dead, on the floor of the smoke-filled cave. The back of his head was all burst open and chunks of white bone and multicolored brain fragments hung out like the insides of a pumpkin.

I left Reg in the cave and went to attend to Boston Steve and Renoir. When I got back to the site where I'd left them, Renoir was already dead. Bled out. A pool of dark red blood surrounded his unmoving form. His hands were covered in blood, too. Guess I hit something more vital than his cock and he'd tried to stem the flow. Boston Steve gasped against a boulder, moaning in pain, eyes closed. He didn't even know I was there until I slit his throat with my Bowie knife. His eyes looked up at me, his life gushing and bubbling from his throat and onto his chest. Then, his eyes looked up at the sky, and he slumped back before his pupils finally rolled, lifeless, up into his head so I could only see the whites. I wiped my knife on his coat. Boston Steve was finally good for something.

It took me a while, but I stripped their bodies for belongings. I took the ammo but left their shitty guns, except for one of the rifles. Food, water, and cigarettes—I took it all, even if I wasn't going to be using it personally. Most everything had trading value these days. One by one, I dragged their half-naked corpses into the cave and piled them together in the corner. While doing so, to my surprise, I found a skeleton in the opposite end of the cavern. Rags of leftover clothing still clung to the ribs. A worn leather book was nearby on a rock ledge. Its left foot was missing, and it looked like the person had been shot in the side with a shotgun at some point. An old, dust-covered .45 lay on the ground by its remaining foot. When I looked at the left side of the skull, there was a big fuckin' hole in it.

"Allow me to introduce to *you*, Mr. Bones, three formerly-rude cocksuckers with all the grace of a pile of shit—who now, in death, are agreeable enough for company. At least more so than they were while living their miserable fuckin' lives."

Mr. Bones said nothing in reply. I grabbed the book from the ledge and blew the dust from its cover and spine. It was small. I opened the first page. Several pages in front were ripped out and missing.

If you're reading this, I don't know whether to congratulate you on not being dead or to feel sorry for you for still being alive. My name is Peter Harvey, and in case you've found this book, I'm probably really close nearby.

I looked up from the pages and back to the skeleton. The eye sockets were gaping and the mouth open in an eternal grin. Tufts of hair still clung to shreds of scalp. *Peter Harvey*, I thought. *Nice to make your fuckin' acquaintance.*

I closed the book and looked out at the sky. The clouds were rolling in, and the sun would be setting soon. No time for me to make it anywhere else tonight. In the morning, I would head back to the hideout and grab some more supplies and then figure out where to go from there. I turned around to look again at the bones of Peter Harvey and the three bodies of Renoir, Reg, and Boston Steve.

"Well, Mr. Peter Harvey. Guess tonight you and I are going to get acquainted. But first, I need to build a fuckin' fire, if you'll be so kind as to excuse my fuckin' rudeness."

I stared a long while at Peter's empty eye sockets, but of course he didn't jump back to life and start laying into me about my use of colorful language. I liked this man.

The fire didn't take me long to build. There wasn't much in the way of fuel near the cave mouth, but I walked into the remnants of the tree line and picked what I could use from there. I settled on a spot near the cave mouth and watched the falling rain dot the granite until the rocks became slick. The wind picked up, so I grabbed a blanket from the leftover supplies and wrapped myself in it, stoking the flames with a stick. I couldn't see the corpses in the back of the cave, but I lifted Peter Harvey's journal into the light of the fire as if to show the skeleton who was once a man that I was ready to read about his trials and tribulations.

"Well," I said, looking into the darkness where the dead men lay, "here we fuckin' go."

I opened the journal and resumed where I'd left off before.

I'm guessing you probably know about The Collapse. How could you not? At the time, I remember thinking it was nothing. I mean, we'd already lived through the Y2K bug and the end of the world as predicted by the Mayan calendar. Every year, it seemed like there was a new apocalypse to watch out for. But this was the real deal.

When The Blackout happened, people were scared out of their minds. Planes dropped out of the sky. Massive accidents on the highways. Power plants overloaded. We didn't know it was global, and we didn't know that the government had known it was going to happen and were prepared. We didn't know that our own people would be so quick to put us into body bags. But they were.

The looters are the ones who kicked things off. Small mobs at first, mostly in the bigger cities. They went around tearing things up. Smashing store fronts, flipping cars. Neighborhoods banded together, worked with what was left of the police force. Curfews were imposed, violence escalated. They moved from tear gas and rubber bullets to fully-automatic weaponry and military hardware – at least what was still working.

My wife Melissa and I lived in a little A-frame house built back in the 1930's. It was a fixer-upper, for sure, but she'd bought it before we'd met. If it'd been my choice, we would have moved, but her folks lived just two houses down and she would never have moved too far away from them. Her family was pretty close-knit, unlike my own.

So, when The Blackout did happen, my wife and I kept a pretty low profile. I was from New Hampshire, so I was used to the power being out in the winter for long periods of time. But Melissa and her family had come all the way to Barning, Vermont, from Studio City, California. They weren't used to the cold like I was.

We kept thinking that the power would come back on soon. It had to. Well, according to some people who'd tried to tell us what was going on, there was a crazy series of solar flares happening. The first ones weren't too bad. The ones after, those were worse. The heat rose even though it was winter. Buildings caught on fire. Trees. We didn't even get the worst of it. Barning, and much of the northeast, actually, was spared due to the colder climates. The south burned up. The west. Everyone who survived came to the northeast, but there weren't too many survivors.

For a long time, we suffered. Ash went up into the sky and covered the earth for a while. We called that the Year Without Seasons. The government tried to come back in and impose order, but what was left were a bunch of roving bands of killers and people murdering and stealing to survive. I was one of those people.

You see, if you're reading this—could you do me a favor? I left Melissa back in Barning. I thought for sure we were all going to die. Her parents died of starvation. Some gangs were going around, demanding that all grown men in the area join them or be executed. I was scared, I was selfish. I'd seen them dump lamp oil all over one poor bastard and light him up. He covered his face with his hands, as if that was going to stave off the flames, but his skin started bubbling and popping, along with the muscle and fat under it, like a pork chop in a cast iron skillet. He kneeled down and then his muscles started retracting from the heat until his arms came down to his sides and his blackened face looked up to heaven. His jawbone had split and was hanging off the right side of his face, charred and burnt. I couldn't get that image out of my head. It just kept replaying over and over and over, and I could even see it when I shut my eyes. I still can, right now. The last thing I wanted was to burn alive, like so many others had done, so I ran from there. I didn't want to burn, you see? Barning seemed mostly safe, aside from the gangs, but I just couldn't do it. The sun didn't burn everything up as much as other places, but the people did. Which is kind of ironic, actually. Kind of like what I'm about to do.

In fact, if you're reading this, I've already decided to blow my own brains out. Better that than what's waiting for me in this crazy new world. I hope Melissa does the same before she's raped or murdered or starves to death.

So, if you find this, if you've read my little confession—know that I'm not a terrible person. I've done terrible, cowardly things. But I loved Melissa, and I still love her. It's just that love isn't enough anymore. Maybe it never was. I wish we had been born in a different time. Other people got to live out their lives peacefully. Have kids, settle down. We had the special luck of the sun burning all that up in less than a couple of months. Tell Melissa that I'm sorry, that I love her. Tell her mostly that I'm sorry, though. Maybe, if we're lucky, there's something greater out there after we're gone? Maybe we can meet somewhere up in the clouds and joke about all this. Maybe you'll meet us up there, too, stranger. Goodbye.

—PH

I didn't know what to say after what I'd read. I closed the journal, threw it in the fire. The pages curled up first, and then the cover and spine.

"No. You're not getting out of things that easy, you gutless cock-sucker," I said, squeezing my fists as tight as I could.

I spit into the fire and the saliva sizzled and dissipated. I put out the flames after a while and tried my best to sleep, tossing and turning as I always did. Nightmares were a constant factor in my life, and this night was no different, despite my small victory. Maybe it was even made worse. I dreamed Reggie and the boys raped me. That one almost made me throw up. I dreamed that my father stabbed my mother to death. I had many small nightmares that night, and each one woke me up in a panic. In the final nightmare, I dreamed that I was sitting in a saloon with Peter Harvey. He had no face, only a skull, the back of it blown out like Reggie's. He lifted his glass to toast me, and then when I only stared at him in response, he chugged the liquor, and I watched it spill through his empty mandibles and non-existent throat, onto the dirty floor. A puddle of alcohol soon formed at his skeletal feet. In my dream, I tossed a lit cigarette into the spilled libations and Peter Harvey and his stool went up in flames. His skeleton contorted in the way he'd described the other man doing in his journal, and in my dream, I smiled. He screamed.

When I woke for the last time, the first thing I did was move to the back of the cave and hoist Peter Harvey's skeleton from its seated position. Dust rose in plumes, and I held my breath as I placed the bones on top of the other corpses. Flies had already started to commence their grotesque party on the bodies. I grabbed one of the lanterns Renoir had kept in his pack and smashed it, emptying the oil on the pile of dead cowards, including Peter Harvey, and then smoked a cigarette until it was just a nub. I dumped some of Renoir's artwork on the pile of corpses for good measure.

"Peter Harvey, you're as much a cocksucker as the likes of these godless sons of bitches. Burn with them. If I see Melissa's kin in Barning, I'll tell them I did them a fuckin' favor by burning you like should've been done back then."

I took the nub of lit tobacco from my chapped lips and threw it on the lantern oil. It started to smoke, and then finally erupted in a small blaze which consumed hair, cloth, fingernails, and Renoir's drawings of titties, until the whole pile grew into a massive pyre. I took everything I could carry and set out from the cave as it filled with smoke and the smell of burning men.

"Barning, Vermont. Hope you're ready for me, cocksuckers."

I didn't know where this town was, nor if it was still standing, but I didn't have anywhere else to go. Never did, I suppose. It was worth a look, if only to sate my own fuckin' curiosity.

When I arrived back at the hideout I used to share with Reggie and the bunch, I loaded up one of the horses and grabbed a couple of maps. There was one for New England and a more detailed one for Vermont, both of them curled with age. I found the town of Barning nestled in between two mountains: Gary Mountain and Goose Mountain. With one gloved finger, I traced a circle around the name of the town. Looked like I could follow one of the old highways for most of the way, and then I'd have to figure something else out.

As I began to ride off in the direction of Vermont, I wondered how Melissa Harvey had met her own end, and I hoped she'd lived as normal a life as she could, despite everything. Some fuckin' help her husband had been. I stopped and spun the horse around, and I took one last look at the cave, which was now billowing with black smoke. I took my hat off and held it to my chest. I stroked the horse's mane—his name was Barnaby—and he whinnied in response.

"Adios, y'bunch of cocksuckers," I said, digging my heels into Barnaby's sides. We sped off in search of greener pastures.

Barnaby was my only fuckin' companion the entire way to what they used to call Vermont. He was a good horse, and that was something in these times. Good animals were hard to come by, what with all the fuckin' fires burning up everything all the time. Luckily, the damned thing subsisted well enough on whatever grass and straw we happened upon, and that was about all we encountered on our ride for miles and miles. Great for Barnaby, but not so fuckin' great for me. We made our way through a busted little town called Exeter while we were riding through New Hampshire. I thought I saw some people peeking their heads out a few windows, but they didn't bother me any, and it's a good thing too because I'd have shot those cocksuckers just as soon as talk to them. There were people, or what used to be people, who stalked the hills, sometimes on all fours, and if you wanted to live you had to shoot them all on fuckin' sight or they'd swarm you. There was no telling who was gonna try to rob and murder you, so may as well shoot every damned one of them.

We stopped at an old gazebo in the center of Exeter by a crumbling courthouse for a rest and some quick lunch. I dug around in the saddlebags and remembered I'd taken some jerky from Renoir's satchel before I burned him up. The jerky wasn't bad, but I hoped we'd find something more substantial on the way. We went along after that, riding close to some old train tracks that, according to the map, looked like they went up through Massachusetts into some city called Pittsfield, right before it opened up into New York State. I was taking the long way, that was for fuckin' sure, but I didn't want to risk taking the main roads and getting chased by gangs or marauders.

I passed the time by singing softly to my fuckin' self, since Barnaby wasn't doing anything to chip in, except it sounded like he was snickerin' a couple times at my terrible voice. My grandma, her name was Debbie, used to sing us songs from the old days, back before The Burn, back when she was a kid. Grandma Debbie was such a pure soul, not meant for a world like the one we got. She was always feeding what stray animals or sick animals happened upon our home, even when we had nothing. She wasn't much for singing, either, but it didn't matter because whenever she sang, she kept a smile on her face, and that always made me smile. I couldn't even remember the last time I smiled.

One song I really liked. I couldn't remember none of the words to it, but the melody stuck with me. Grandma said it was a song called "Take On Me" or "Take Me On" or something like that. May as well have been called Take a Shit because I couldn't fuckin' remember for the life of me what the words actually were, but the melody made me calm, and it had a sweetness to it that made me think of a time in my fuckin' life when I wasn't subjected to so much damned sadness and loneliness. Back before The Burn and The Collapse, things must have been so much easier. Everyone probably shit daffodils and fucked each other for free and not for food.

Me and Barnaby came up over a rise. We still had quite a ways to go, but in the distance, I could see what people used to call the Green Mountains stretching out before us. Except they weren't green anymore, if they ever had been. They were brown lumps of rock and dirt strewn all over with dead, dry wood ripe for the next big burn that would eventually come in a few years. Barnaby and me picked our way through the hills, stopping when we needed to rest. It had been about ten days since we'd set out. We'd taken our fuckin' time, that's for sure. We only had about nine or ten days' ride according to the map.

Two days after that is when the hill people came for us.

I'm not sure where the sons of bitches picked up our scent, but Barnaby smelled them coming long before I fuckin' laid eyes on them. His ears perked up as he trotted down an old service road through the Green Mountains. We'd been following some sickly, poor excuse for a trickling river when ol' Barnaby whipped his head around and snorted, pawing at the ground. I'd known Barnaby long enough not to question his senses, because even though he was a damned horse, he was smarter than almost every other human fuckin' being I ever saw.

"Easy, boy," I said, patting his mane. He gave me an appreciative snort and kept his ears perked. I unholstered Betsy and cocked her, resting the barrel on my left forearm for a steady firing position as I used that arm to hold the reins. I turned Barnaby around to see if I could see any of the cocksuckers in the trees, but I couldn't spot a one of them. Barnaby was getting more agitated by the fuckin' minute, so I turned again, and we rode fast next to the stream. That's when shots started popping off all around us and there came a great whooping and hollering from the scrub brush and vines.

I saw a blur of motion as a dirty, lanky, tall man with a bowl cut burst from the bushes. He had a rusty saw blade attached to the end of a baseball bat, and I pulled the trigger on Betsy, and she let him have it. The man spun around with the force of the blast and twisted somewhere out of sight as I rode on. I heard bullets whizzing by me like angry mosquitos. I was worried Barnaby was gonna be struck by a stray shot, so I turned and fired behind me, creating a small smoke screen as I rode faster. After about twenty minutes of hard riding, I didn't hear the hill people anymore, but I didn't want to create a false sense of fuckin' security, so I turned Barnaby into the river, and we rode through it for a few miles before jumping out on the bank and riding on the road again. I was fairly confident the cocksuckers wouldn't be able to follow us, inbred as they looked to be, but when we stopped to rest, I made sure to only sleep a couple hours before we set off again.

Before long, I realized we were almost in Barning. I still didn't know why exactly I'd risked so much and traveled all this way. For all I fuckin' knew, it was no longer there or was packed full of inbred hillfolk or the sun-poisoned cocksuckers that lived underground. Or maybe it was even a town full of people like Renoir, Boston Steve, and Reggie Durham. Most towns were full of cocksuckers like them, but, every once in a while, there seemed to be an oasis, though they were few and far between.

The final night before I knew I'd reach Barning, I stayed up late, unable to sleep. I pet Barnaby's snout and scratched behind his ear, and he stood there sleeping soundly as I gazed up at the night sky. I finally lay down and hummed Grandma's song until I dozed off.

I didn't bother eating anything for breakfast. My stomach was in knots. Barnaby seemed to sense it, and he picked up his pace the last few miles until I saw smoke on the horizon and what looked like a town rising up out of the morning haze. We stayed a few miles away from town, and I looked through my binoculars at the people milling around. We made wide circles around the perimeter until I noticed what looked to be a big church on the outskirts. The people I saw through the lenses seemed generally harmless, but that didn't mean a fuckin' thing.

The sun was starting to come out and both me and Barnaby were going to want some shade soon, so I spurred him toward the back side of the church, where there was an old graveyard. The town didn't seem to have any guards out this way, and I saw the burnt and rusted hull of a truck outside the church. I tied Barnaby to an old fence in the shade of the building while Betsy and I investigated what looked like a scorched skeleton clutching the remains of an urn. I turned back to look at Barnaby, and he rocked his head slightly and let out a small whinny.

I set up shop in the old church. There was a sign on the inside that read *First Baptist Church of Barning*. There were strangely no bodies on the inside, but a fine layer of ash and dust coated everything. I made sure to feed and water Barnaby, and I eventually moved him inside the church to get away from the fuckin' sun during its hottest time of day. From the shade, I watched the townsfolk through my binoculars.

During my time watching the people of Barning go about their business, I noticed something that let me drop my guard a little bit. Some of them were fuckin' smiling. I couldn't remember the last time a smile had crossed my lips, aside from maybe when I shot one of those cocksuckers back at the cave. But these were real smiles. Sure, they looked dirty and desperate like anyone else in the fuckin' world right now, but it looked like maybe they still had some hope.

That night, I decided that the very next day I would introduce my fuckin' self. I lay next to Barnaby in the old church. I'd found some old broom to sweep away the dust in a corner of the room, and I started to drift off. That's when I remembered the words to the song. It *was* "Take on Me." I could hear my Grandma Debbie singing it to me as a young girl. I pictured her dark curls and bright eyes and her unforgettable smile.

I closed my eyes to sleep, and wouldn't you know it? A fuckin' smile played across my face just before I drifted off.

About the Authors

Franklin Ard's writing blurs many genres, from science fiction, fantasy, and mystery to magical realism and Southern gothic. Over the years, his fiction and poetry has appeared in numerous venues, such as *Nightmare Magazine, Tales, Sherlock Holmes Mystery Magazine, Suspense Magazine,* and *Deep Magic.* He is a graduate of Clarion West Writers Workshop and the University of Southern Maine's Stonecoast MFA program. Additionally, he holds a doctorate in Educational Leadership from the University of South Alabama, where he oversees the university's Center for Academic Excellence. Formerly Editor-in-Chief of *Oracle Fine Arts Review* and Managing Editor of *Stonecoast Review,* he now serves as Editor-in-Chief of Rogue Owl Press and lead copy editor at Headless Hydra Press. He resides in Mobile, Alabama, with his wife and son, where they enjoy the humid frog weather. Find him online at www.franklinard.com.

Joseph Carro holds an MFA from Stonecoast at the University of Southern Maine. He is the co-author of *The Little Coffee Shop of Horrors* anthology and has served as an editor and proofreader for the Glyphs Productions line of comic books since 2015. He has written for *itcherMag* and can generally be found engaging in some sort of geeky/nerdy activity throughout the day. Oh, and he was also in a movie with Kelsey Grammer (and will say that every chance he gets). He currently resides in Woodford, Vermont, inside the infamous Bennington Triangle, although he'll always be a Mainer at heart.

Paul Carro was born and raised in Maine, where he was published at an early age in an anthology of Maine authors alongside one of his horror icons. After college, he left the lakes of Maine for the oceans of Cali-fornia, where he toiled for years in the film/TV industry before recent-ly returning to his literary roots. A longtime comic book and horror nerd, he now writes novels featuring both his passions. When not writ-ing, he can be found hiking all over California.

Shane R. Collins is the owner of Headless Hydra Press, a tabletop gaming company that creates accessories and supplements for roleplaying games. His work has appeared in *The Master's Review* in an issue that won the IndieFab Silver Medal for Best Short Story Collection. Shane lives in rural Vermont with his wife and their assorted pets and children.

Renee S. DeCamillis is a horror editor and the author of the psycho-logical thriller/supernatural horror/bizarro novella *The Bone Cutters*, published through Eraserhead Press. She is a member of the Horror Writers Association, the New England Horror Writers, and the Horror Writers of Maine. Renee is also a songwriter, musician, singer, and a tree-hugging hippie with a sharp metal edge. Renee's short fiction appears in the *Wicked Women* anthology from NEHW Press, *Northern Frights, The Journal of Horror Writers of Maine 25—Mud Season 2021, lost, Deadman's Tome: The Conspiracy Issue, Siren's Call eZine* Issue 37: the 6th Annual Women in Horror Month Edition, and *The Other Stories Podcast.* Her poetry appears in

The Horror Writers Association Po-etry Showcase Volume IV. Her first c omic b ook i s a lso forthcoming from Phi3 Comics. Renee earned her B.A. in psychology from the Uni-versity of Southern Maine and her MFA in Popular Fiction from the Stonecoast program. She also attended Berklee College of Music as a music business major with guitar as her principal instrument. Renee is a former model, school rock band teacher, creative writing teacher, private guitar instructor, A&R representative for an indie record label, therapeutic mentor, psychological technician, and preschool teacher. She is also a former gravedigger; she can get rid of a body fast without leaving a trace, and she is not afraid of getting her hands dirty. Renee lives in the woods of southern Maine with her husband, their son, and a house full of ghosts. Visit her online at reneesdecamillis.com. Facebook: Renee S. DeCamillis Author. Instagram: @renee_s._decamillis. Twitter: @ReneeDeCamillis.

Devin Gaither lives on the Mar-Lu Ridge of the Blue Ridge Mountains in Jefferson, MD with her dog, Pippa. She is a Business Analyst by trade and is also the Aerial Arts Program Director for Luna Aerial Dance & Performing Arts in Frederick, MD. Additionally, she enjoys mak-ing time for creating stained glass artwork (Mar-Lu Glassworks) and laboring over math puzzles. Devin earned her MFA in Creative Writ-ing from Stonecoast at the University of Southern Maine. In 2022, she was selected as one of the Top 50 Young Professionals Under 40 by the Frederick County Office of Economic Development.

Derek B. Hoffman i s a g raduate o f t he S tonecoast M FA p rogram at the University of Southern Maine. He is a freelance author, editor, and tutor. For over thirty years, he's authored works ranging from slip-stream poetry, to stories supporting abused children, to inspiring young adult and transmedia odysseys. He also leverages his writing skills as CEO of Veracity by Design, LLC, where he composes, edits, and designs award-winning websites, translates technology into understandable user tutorials, and publishes in peer-reviewed medical journals as part of research projects performed at leading universities. During the day, he resides with his wife and three boys in Austin, TX. At night, he ventures into the fifth co rner of hi s mi nd, cr afting an ever-growing collection of multiverse tales and adventures. Find him online soon at www.derekbhoffman.com.

Rebecca McKenna teaches English literature and writing to high school students, whom she finds qu i te i n teresting an d en g aging. She has been a professional mapmaker for almost two decades and has spent a lifetime loving maps and creating them for her enjoyment. A graduate of the Stonecoast MFA Program at the University of South-ern Maine and a charter member of the Tiny Chair Writing Coopera-tive, she lives in eastern Maine with her husband and misses her kids, who have grown up.

Karen Marie Menzel (neé Bovenmyer) earned an MFA in Creative Writing from the University of Southern Maine in 2013. Her first novel debuted from Dreamspinner Press in 2017. Her novellas, short sto-ries, and poems appear in more than 40 publications, and she is an Escape Artists' Mothership Zeta and Pseudopod editorial staff alumna. Teaching and mentoring writers at Iowa State University and Western Technical college brings her great joy. Find her online at www.karen-bovenmyer.com.

Richard Squires is a writer, editor, and musician living in New Jersey. His fiction has appeared in *The MacGuffin*, *Jewish Literary Journal*, and *BigCityLit*, among other publications, and he has book reviews forthcoming in *American Book Review*. Richard is the owner of LifeStory (www.LifeStoryMemoir.com), a company that writes people's memoirs for them, creating legacies their families cherish for generations. A proud member of the Tiny Chair Writing Cooperative, Richard earned his MFA from Stonecoast at the University of Southern Maine.

Chloe Viner was born in Louisiana and raised in Cambridge, Massachusetts. She graduated from Bates College with a B.A. in philosophy. Chloe attended Vermont Law School, where she graduated with a J.D. and master's degree in Environmental Law and Policy. Her passion for helping others led her away from the legal system and into social work, and she now works as the Executive Director at Bennington County Coalition for the Homeless. In her spare time, Chloe is a poet and artist. She has authored four books of poetry, and two of her murals are on display at the Saint Albans Museum. Chloe lives in Woodford, Vermont, with her husband, twin four-year-olds, and assorted pets.

Acknowledgements

The editors and writers wish to extend our sincerest thanks the following backers for their support of the initial Kickstarter campaign, which made possible the production of this book:

Andrea Adams, Agustin, Julie Alviar, Chad Auld, Melanie B., Ian Bannon, Stephanie Barton, Rachel and Doug Beck, Randy P. Belanger, Alison Beman, Julia Benson-Slaughter, Carl Blair, Howard Blakeslee, Matt Blanchette, Jeff Bleam, Nan Boury, Sam Brillhart, Jim Brownrigg, Steven Byrd, Nova C., Jamie Cismoski, Eric L. Collette, Joshua Lee Cooper, Niki Coppola, Justin Alexander Dorsey, MaryEllen Durkin, Sarah Eriksen, David Evers, Chilton Festwick III, Sadie Fitzgerald, Tracy "Rayhne" Fretwell, Peter Gailitis, Mary Gaitan, Devin Gaither, Phyllis Gibson, Robin Ginther-Venneri, Casey Griffith, Carol Gyzander, Victor P. HaerinckJr., Rachel Halpern, Daniel Hanson-Brown, The Hardiman Family, Headless Hydra Press, Robert Heil, Joshua Hengel, Marsha Ingles, Pam Joplin, Anika Kastelic, Lori-Ane Kiernan, The LaBounta Family, Samantha Landström, Luis Leal, Tim MacKay, Tyler Manship, Debbie McLean, Lisa McLemore, Torin Micklus, Neon Pixxius, Linda Niehoff, Richard O'Shea, Cristine Patrick, Steve Pattee, Pippa, Tony Pisculli, Salvatore L. Puma, Jan Rasch, Diego Riley, Erick Rivas, Jason Roush, Ruthenia, Ryan Scarcella, Guy Schmidt, Anthea Sharp, Katherine Shipman, John Smith, Amy Smith, Kelly Snyder, Georgia Stahl, Nicholas Stephenson, Adam "Chili" Stevens, Jordan Theyel, Thorsten, Nathan Turner, Ben Warner, WarOrdos, Thad Watulak, Matthew Webb, Joe Williams, Alison Wogatske, Lillian F. Wolfe, Eron Wyngarde, and Zian.

Special Thanks from Rogue Owl Press to:

Stephanie Evers Ard for her great ideas and constant support, encouragement, and love.

Joseph Carro for his steadfast belief in the potential of Barning and the writers involved in this project.

The authors for their patience, dedication, and energy over many years from initial idea to final product—including contributing their time and creative works during the Kickstarter campaign.

Rebecca McKenna for going above and beyond—in ways too numerous to count—to help bring this project to life.

Tiny Chair Writing Cooperative for the motivation, humor, and incredible friendship.

Veracity by Design for exceptional website development and graphic design services.

Hanscom Construction for generously allowing the use of their large-scale printing facilities.

Note to Readers

We invite you to join the Rogue Owl Press Readers' Club! Be the first to know when new books are published, as well as receive updates about discounts, free books, and special events. Join here:

www.rogueowlpress.com/join

Did you enjoy this Rogue Owl Press title? Please consider leaving a review at your favorite online bookstore. Reviews help other readers discover great books!

About the Publisher

Rogue Owl Press publishes *startling stories*. We're drawn to writing that is entertaining, exciting, and captivating, while simultaneously powerful, complex, and genre-bending.

We publish works that stop us, as readers, in our tracks—that jolt us in astonishing ways. We seek writing that makes us ponder the universe from a new angle and provides an opening to fall into another reality. In the words of Jack Kerouac, we want to feel everything all at once.

Startling stories transcend any one genre, style, or storytelling philosophy. A startling work of art may color within the lines of genre conventions, or it may blur those lines—or defy expectations altogether. But such works all have one thing in common: their beating hearts.

Startling stories are indeed alive.

Find Rogue Owl Press online at **www.rogueowlpress.com**

www.ingramcontent.com/pod-product-compliance
Lightning Source LLC
Chambersburg PA
CBHW020631250626
47154CB00008B/2623